An Unexpected Arrangement

Heidi McCahan

LOVE INSPIRED

INSPIRATIONAL ROMANCE

LOVE INSPIRED®
INSPIRATIONAL ROMANCE

Recycling programs for this product may not exist in your area.

ISBN-13: 978-1-335-48864-0

An Unexpected Arrangement

Copyright © 2020 by Heidi Blankenship

This edition published by arrangement with Harlequin Books S.A.

For questions and comments about the quality of this book, please contact us at CustomerService@Harlequin.com.

Love Inspired
22 Adelaide St. West, 40th Floor
Toronto, Ontario M5H 4E3, Canada
www.Harlequin.com

Printed in U.S.A.

This I recall to my mind, therefore have I hope. It is of the Lord's mercies that we are not consumed, because his compassions fail not. They are new every morning: great is thy faithfulness.

—*Lamentations* 3:21–23

For Jill Lynn and Lee Tobin McClain: thank you for your kindness and encouragement. This book would not be possible without your pep talks and inspirational brainstorming sessions.

Chapter One

It was official: he was getting a puppy.

Jack Tomlinson waited at the counter in Angie's Diner and stared at the photo on his phone of two golden-haired puppies lined up on a plaid bed, their brown eyes staring back at him. Even his frigid, closed-off heart couldn't help melting a little. His brother, Drew, had sent him the picture a few weeks ago, and before he could talk himself out of it, he'd texted Laramie and arranged to stop by and visit today. The puppies wouldn't be available for another three weeks, but hopefully he could pick the one he wanted.

Then he'd have a new puppy by the Fourth of July and his thirtieth birthday. Maybe a pet would help him cope with the guilt and regret he couldn't seem to shake. The loss of his father on the heels of Uncle Kenny's suicide had wrecked him. And he couldn't forget the irresponsible behavior that had followed. All the stupid choices he'd made in the last three years, trying to numb the pain.

"Your order's ready." Sandra, the petite redheaded waitress, set a take-out container on the counter. The aroma of his usual breakfast—ham-and-cheese omelet with a side of bacon—made his stomach growl. Jack tucked his phone in his pocket, grabbed his food and followed Sandra toward the register.

"Where you off to in such a hurry?" Pete Fisher, a regular at the diner and one of his late father's closest friends, sat with three of his buddies in a booth nearby.

"I have a meeting." Jack kept walking. He didn't have the time or the patience to sit with the retired wheat farmers of Merritt's Crossing. The conversation always circled back to the same old topic—Jack's career choice. He was over it.

"Is that right?" Jack felt Pete's gaze lingering as he pulled out his wallet. "You know, it's not too late for you to start building furniture. You've probably got all the tools you need in that woodshop you inherited. Then you wouldn't have to spend so much time away from home."

Jack hesitated, a ten-dollar bill outstretched. There it was. The advice Pete offered almost every time he saw Jack in the diner. Which was often, since Jack bought his breakfast at Angie's at least four times a week. Not that he was interested in listening to Pete. Or anyone else. Building furniture was the last thing he wanted to do.

Sandra offered an empathetic smile as she took his money. Jack pretended to ignore Pete and the rest of the men at the table. Let them talk. He already had a great job. His position as a cybersecurity analyst kept him busy and required frequent trips out of state, which was a bonus. He *liked* traveling. The more time he spent away from Merritt's Crossing, the less he had to deal with other people's ridiculous expectations about how he should live his life. The Tomlinson family furniture business was better off without him. He'd heard the gossip and the not-so-subtle whispers around town. *It's a real shame about Jack and his dad. Those Tomlinson men had their fair share of fights. If they'd been getting along, things might be different.*

He'd give anything to go back and undo his last conversation with his father.

"Have a great day, fellas." Jack dropped the change from Sandra in the tip jar, flashed Pete and the gang a tight smile, then strode toward the exit. The warm May sunshine greeted him as he stepped outside. While the diner's door swung closed, he couldn't shake Pete's words.

It's not too late...you've probably got all the tools you need. Pete was right about that. The woodshop behind the house Jack had bought from Aunt Willa and his cousin McKenna was filled with tools from his father and Uncle Kenny. Not that he had any plans to use those tools or to build furniture. Ever. Dad and Uncle Kenny had encouraged him, but the furniture business had destroyed their relationship, so why would Jack get involved? He and his father had had a terrible argument about Jack's lack of interest in carrying the family's legacy. Those harsh words were the last Jack had spoken to his dad before he died in a car accident. The pain still knifed at him every time he thought about their horrible fight.

But he still wasn't interested in building furniture or giving up his career in cybersecurity.

Jack stole a glance down Main Street at the Tomlinson's Furniture building. A delivery truck was parked out front and his sister, Skye, and brother-in-law, Gage, were speaking to the driver. Jack turned away. Skye had rescued the store from financial ruin and business was great now. She didn't need him. So maybe he'd helped his father and uncle build a table or two back in the day. That hardly made him a professional. He strode toward his truck, eager to eat his breakfast and forget Pete's annoying commentary. Late last night, he'd read about a cybersecurity job in Utah and he planned to apply. It was time to get out of Merritt's Crossing and escape the heartache and the expectations he would never live up to.

After eating alone in his truck with the air-conditioning cranked, Jack tossed the empty container on the floorboards in front of the passenger seat, then sent Laramie a text message that he was on his way.

Laramie was Skye's best friend and one of the few people in his life who didn't pressure him to change careers. Not that they'd spent much time talking lately. He didn't even know she'd started a dog breeding business. He thought he knew everything about everyone in their small, eastern Colorado town, but this was news to him.

Then again, she was invited to their family gatherings and he'd made excuses to avoid almost all of them. Jack hadn't spent more than five minutes with Laramie since Easter, and that was more than a month ago. Laramie was smart, beautiful and kind. He'd had a huge crush on her when he was a teenager. Just the other night, one of Gage's friends had asked if Laramie was single, and had tried to get Jack to give him her phone number. He'd felt oddly possessive of Laramie in the moment, since the guy didn't strike him as someone who was right for her.

Jack winced and scrubbed his fingertips along his jaw. Not that he had any business judging anyone else. His last brief relationship had confirmed what he'd long suspected—he was a mess. And not ready for a serious commitment. Maybe he wasn't ready for a pet, either. Jack drummed his thumb against the steering wheel and considered bailing on the puppy plan.

Don't be an idiot.

He could stop a hacker from infiltrating a network and banish cybersecurity threats, but he couldn't accept responsibility for a puppy? Disgusted at his cowardly behavior, he mashed the accelerator and merged onto the highway headed toward Laramie's house.

He wasn't giving up on his mission. Sure, a puppy was an odd way to add balance to his life, but at least he was trying. More than anything, Jack longed to climb out of this hole he'd created and start fully living again. While he couldn't change the mistakes in his past, he was tired of letting his regret shackle him. Keeping him isolated and a prisoner to the shame he couldn't escape. Caring for another of God's creations was a first step.

"Jack Tomlinson wants a puppy?" Laramie Chambers stared at the detailed notes her unofficial intern, Hope, had left on the kitchen table. While Hope was only a junior in high school, she was also Laramie's starting setter on the volleyball team, a small group leader for teens at church and the best student in the junior class that Laramie taught. When Hope had approached Laramie and asked for advice on setting up an internship with a small business owner, Laramie had quickly arranged for Hope to help launch her brand-new dog breeding business.

Laramie hadn't planned on keeping a litter of puppies in her spare bedroom or owning any kind of small business. But she also hadn't expected her grandfather's health to deteriorate so quickly. The strong, independent wheat farmer was getting belligerent and confused. He was too much for Grandma to manage, and Laramie and her parents were worried about keeping Grandma and Grandpa safe.

However, her big plans had spontaneously imploded when the first litter produced only two puppies. After expenses, there wouldn't be much money left over to give her grandmother. It wasn't nearly enough to make a dent in her grandfather's expenses at a memory care facility, but she had to do something.

Laramie's stomach knotted tight when she thought about her grandparents' struggles and the exorbitant cost of adequate care. Her parents were trying their best to manage the farm and care for her grandparents, but the stress was taking its toll. The nearest decent facility was over an hour away in Denver. Even if she scrimped and saved, her teaching salary and coaching stipend didn't leave her with a lot of extra money every month. When her friends from college offered to help her get started with breeding dogs, Trixie's puppies had become the solution to her family's overwhelming problem, and it looked like they'd found a way to afford the care that Grandpa so desperately needed. Convincing Grandma to accept financial assistance and move Grandpa away from the family farm was going to be an epic battle, but Laramie refused to worry about that now.

She peeked out her kitchen window as Jack's pickup truck eased into her driveway, then glanced at the two goldendoodle puppies currently asleep beside their mother, Trixie, on her dog bed nearby. Hope's notes weren't wrong. Jack had arrived right on time. Laramie couldn't imagine why he thought he needed a pet. He was rarely home, always working and had looked downright miserable the last time she saw him. Not to mention he hadn't been helpful when his own mother needed care after her knee replacement surgery. How was he going to nurture a baby animal?

Boots thumping on her front steps kept her from grabbing her phone and texting her best friend and Jack's older sister, Skye. What would she think about her brother acquiring a puppy?

Jack knocked softly, and Laramie strode toward the door and opened it. His blue eyes met hers, crinkling at the corners as he flashed a sheepish grin.

"Hey." He tucked his hands in his back pockets, like he dropped by her place all the time to cuddle with puppies. Laramie had fully intended to grill him, but that was before those ruddy cheeks and his angular jaw produced a surprising and unmistakable flutter of attraction in her abdomen.

Totally inappropriate! The internal scolding had little impact on her wandering gaze, which defiantly swept from his handsome features to his gray T-shirt, dark-washed jeans and cowboy boots. Her best intentions were no match for his tall, muscular build filling her doorway, either.

"Hey, Jack." She cleared her throat and tipped her chin up. "What's up?"

His flawless brow creased. "I thought I had an appointment to pick out a puppy?"

"I saw your name on the list." Laramie stepped back and motioned for him to come in. "Are you surprising Gage and Skye with a puppy?"

"No." He linked his arms across his chest, which only emphasized his biceps and chiseled forearms and made Laramie wonder what it would feel like to step into the warmth of his embrace.

Stop. Sure, he was handsome, but he was a mess.

A hot mess, by the way.

She turned away as heat warmed her skin. While she couldn't ignore that her thirty-fifth birthday was right around the corner, and her list of potential prospects for a relationship was short, she had plenty of reasons why Jack wasn't boyfriend material. With his inability to commit, he'd broken more hearts than she could count; he was always traveling for work; and he rarely spent time with his family anymore. None of that added up to the substantial, long-term relationship she longed for.

"I want a dog." Jack walked into the living room and sat on the carpet beside Trixie and her puppies.

"Why?"

He glanced over his shoulder, and she realized she'd said that out loud.

"I mean, you seem like you're busy." Laramie sat on the edge of her paisley-print sofa and tried not to stare as the one with the blue collar licked Jack's outstretched fingers. "Puppies need a lot of attention."

"Well, good, because I have a lot of attention to give." Jack scooped up the wheat-colored male and nestled it against his chest. She didn't even bother trying to avert her gaze. Was there anything more appealing? Laramie faked a cough to smother a contented sigh.

"You have a busy life, too." Jack scratched Trixie behind the ears with his free hand. Trixie stared at him with a look that could only be described as adoration. "How do you have time to start a dog breeding business?"

"Please don't tell my grandmother, but I'm trying to earn some extra money to pay for my grandfather's care. We think it's time for him to move into a memory care facility."

The words tumbled effortlessly from her lips. Well. So much for keeping that a secret.

"Oh no." Jack's expression grew pained. "I'm sorry. I'd heard he wasn't doing well, but I didn't know things had gotten that bad."

"Thank you." She sighed. "I know it's dumb trying to keep a secret in this town, but I'm hoping if I give my grandmother the money, she won't be able to argue."

"Your secret is safe with me." He gave her a compassionate smile. "As long as you'll let me claim this little fella."

Despite her misgivings, Laramie couldn't say no. According to Hope's notes, he'd already paid the required deposit. The money had transferred into her account yesterday. There wasn't a good reason to refuse him, anyway. She couldn't hold his busy lifestyle against him. And more than anything, she wanted Jack to be happy. Genuinely happy. The way she remembered him—laughing and mischievous, without a care in the world. Before his uncle's suicide and father's death had set him on the wrong path.

"All right," she relented. "But if he's more than you can handle, you have to promise to bring him back and let me re-home him. No questions asked."

"I promise." Jack's eyes held hers. She'd never believed all that talk about the space between two people popping and crackling. Until now. The paperwork he needed to sign was in the kitchen. All she needed was his signature. Except she couldn't move. Didn't want to move.

Suddenly the puppy clamped his teeth on Jack's arm, interrupting the moment. Jack flinched and glanced down at the puppy. "Hey, no biting."

"I'll get your contract." Laramie stood and walked

toward the kitchen. Even though she didn't have the husband and family she'd assumed would be hers by now, Jack Tomlinson was not her proverbial Prince Charming. Always attracted to the impulsive, good-looking guys, she'd been left brokenhearted one too many times. She knew better. They were friends. Nothing more.

Jack slowly turned into his driveway, where a white SUV greeted him. His scalp prickled as he punched the button on his garage door opener and then eased his truck into his usual parking spot. He wasn't expecting guests.

He gripped his phone in one hand as he got out of his truck and approached the driver's side of the SUV. The window automatically rolled down to reveal a woman in her midthirties, with dark circles under her eyes and brown hair twisted into a tight bun.

"Are you Jack Tomlinson?"

"Yes. And you are?"

"Miranda Harris. I'm a social worker with the Colorado Division of Child Welfare. Do you know Gwen Hultgren?"

His body flashed hot, then cold. *Gwen.* His gaze flitted past Miranda toward the center row of the SUV. Were those car seats?

"Jack?" Miranda's question required an answer. The car's exhaust fumes stung his nostrils as he tried to draw a deep breath.

"Yeah, yes. I—I know Gwen."

"Have you spoken with her or a member of her family recently?"

Shame heated his skin. He and Gwen had had a brief relationship. Although that was hardly the phrase for their weekend together. Jack shook his head. He'd called once and left a voice mail, but she'd never called back, and he'd stayed away from Nevada.

Miranda stared through the windshield, both hands still gripping the steering wheel. "Jack, you're a father. These babies are yours."

His chest compressed, like a block of wood jammed in the vise grips in his uncle's woodshop. "Babies?"

"Yes. Twin girls. They're six months old."

Right on cue, the sound of a baby cooing filtered toward him. Jack's thoughts churned, desperate to grasp this announcement. It couldn't be true, could it?

He'd lived with the guilt of the seemingly harmless flirting in a hotel elevator that had led to him skipping the tech conference in Nevada and spending three drunken days with a virtual stranger. Gwen. He wasn't proud of his actions. The lingering grief and anger over his father's death had plunged him into a downward spiral of poor choices.

But a pregnancy? Twins? Why hadn't she told him? Where was she now? Why was there a social worker here in his driveway with two babies in her car?

Jack slowly scraped his fingers across his jaw. "Gwen. Where is she?"

Empathy flickered in Miranda's eyes. "I think it would be best if the girls and I came inside. Do you mind?"

"Okay." How could he say no after the news she'd just delivered? Jack stepped back as Miranda turned off the ignition and climbed out of the car.

He forced himself to draw a calming breath although his heart pounded like a freight train thundering across the prairie. He had *daughters*. And no relationship with their mother. This couldn't be happening. There was no way he was equipped to be a single dad of two help-less babies.

Miranda handed him a car seat. "This is Macey. She's sleeping."

He stared at the baby girl wearing gray-and-pink-striped pajamas. Jack's chest expanded as he caught a glimpse of her full cheeks and thick eyelashes.

"Hi, Macey," he whispered, his voice catching.

"And I'll carry Charlotte in." Miranda held the car seat in one hand and slung the strap of a packed bag over her other shoulder.

Macey and Charlotte. Charlotte and Macey. His daughters? Jack shook his head in disbelief as he slowly walked toward his house, careful not to jostle the precious cargo in his care.

Inside, he lowered Macey's car seat to the floor in the middle of his living room. Miranda did the same with Charlotte's car seat. Jack braced his hands on his hips and stared at the twins. Charlotte stared right back, her curious blue eyes sizing him up. His emotions careened from shock and awe to confusion and hurt. If this was all true, why didn't Gwen tell him he was a father?

"You must have a lot of questions." Miranda set her bag on the floor, then sat on his brown leather sofa.

The understatement of the year. "Where is Gwen?"

"I'm sorry to be the one to tell you this, but Gwen passed away unexpectedly three weeks ago. Car accident."

The words landed like a fist in his gut. Gwen was gone. The babies didn't have a mother. He backed up slowly and slumped into his recliner. His vision tunneled and he struggled to formulate a coherent thought.

"I know it's a shock, me showing up on your doorstep and telling you these babies are yours and their mother is gone." Miranda's spine straightened. "Macey and Charlotte have been in an emergency foster care home while we looked for you. The State of Colorado strives for permanent placement with a biological relative as quickly as possible. That's especially important with very young children. The twins need to bond with their father. You."

"Are you sure I'm their dad?" He did the math in his head. The timing was right.

"I have birth certificates and you can do a paternity test." She tugged a folder from the side of the diaper bag. "As far as the state is concerned, if you've passed a background check, don't have any felony convictions, a documented history of child abuse or a compelling reason why you're unfit to parent, then the babies will be placed with you immediately."

"But I'm a stranger to them." Jack choked out the words. And he couldn't be trusted alone with two babies.

"Not for long." Miranda smiled. "They need you, Jack. I'm sorry Gwen chose to keep them from you. But you're all they have."

"What about Gwen's parents? Does she have any siblings?"

"Unfortunately, Gwen's mother is deceased. We haven't been able to reach her father, and her sister has three young children. She'd like to be more helpful, but she just can't." Miranda pulled her car keys from her pocket. "Like I said, you're the girls' closest biological relative."

Panic welled inside. "You're leaving now?"

She nodded. "As soon as I unload the rest of their belongings."

"You can't even stay for a day or two? Help me figure this out?"

"My caseload is heavy. I have four more families to meet with, so I'll be staying at a hotel in Limon for the next two days." She stood and handed him her business card. "You can call me anytime. There's also a toll-free number for twenty-four-hour assistance. I'll be back to check on your progress in about a month."

Jack scrubbed his hand over his face. He didn't have words.

"I've written down detailed instructions about their normal routines. I have a portable crib in the car, along with about three days' worth of formula, diapers and wipes. You'll need to get connected with a pediatrician as soon as possible and talk about introducing solid foods. The birth certificates and immunizations records are in there, too."

"I can't believe this is happening."

"You'll figure it out. People have babies every day." She opened the door. "I'll get the rest of their stuff."

"No, I'll unload your car. I need a minute." Jack stepped outside, sucking in a deep breath. Even though it was almost ninety degrees, icy tentacles of fear slithered through him.

"I'm not ready to be a father. I was doing good to try to care for a dog," he said.

Minutes later, Miranda's taillights disappeared down the drive. Macey's eyes popped open and Charlotte's face contorted. They both began to cry. What a pathetic, mournful sound.

His heart raced. He reached for his phone and glanced at the screen. What a mess he'd made. Who could he call? He didn't dare tell his family. His mom was going to be so upset. Not to mention disappointed. Laramie's number was the first one he scrolled to. Why not? She'd know what to do.

"You changed your mind, didn't you?" Laramie didn't even bother with a greeting. Her voice carried a triumphant tone, too. He probably deserved that.

Jack stared at the wailing babies still nestled in their car seats in the middle of his living room floor.

"Um, no. N-not exactly," he said, hating the tremor in his voice.

"What is that noise?"

"Laramie, I need help."

"Is that a baby crying?"

"Babies. As in two." Jack kept staring and willing his feet to move, but he had no idea what to do to get the crying to stop. Skye and her husband, Gage, had Connor, and Jack had witnessed plenty of his tantrums, but he couldn't recall how they'd defused the situation.

She gasped. "Two? What are you doing with two babies?"

"Please. Just come over. I'll explain when you get here." Jack raked his hand through his hair as he paced.

"Jack, I—"

"Laramie, I can't call anyone else. Please. I'm begging you."

"All right." She sighed. "I'll be there in ten minutes. Do you have diapers and formula?"

Jack glanced at the diaper bag and plastic bin Miranda had brought and tried to remember her instructions. "Enough for a couple of days."

"Do you know how to mix formula?"

He gritted his teeth. "No."

"Then look in their car seats or their diaper bags for

pacifiers. If they have something to suck on, that might help with the crying for a few minutes. I'll show you how to fix a bottle when I get there."

"Okay. I'll look."

"See you soon."

Jack ended the call, relief flooding through him. He tipped his head back and whispered a prayer of thanks toward the ceiling. Between his anger and then his guilt, Jack hadn't bothered conversing with God in quite a while. But it was time to start. Because he was suddenly a father of two and he was in trouble.

Two babies?

Questions zipped through Laramie's mind as she jogged from her Mazda sedan toward Jack's front door. Had he become a guardian for one of his coworkers' children? Was he an emergency foster parent and hadn't told anyone? Did a neighbor have twins that she didn't know about? The fear in his voice when he'd called indicated the babies were a complete surprise.

Jack greeted her with a panicked expression and a wailing baby in his arms.

"Help." He thrust the baby toward her. Laramie glanced at the other baby lying on a blanket in the middle of the living room, clutching the toes of her footed pajamas and her face pink with anger. Wow, she was really screaming.

"Oh my." Laramie cradled the little girl against her chest and made a shushing sound. "What's her name?"

"That's Macey." Jack closed the door behind her, then walked toward the sofa, which was covered with more blankets, baby clothes and packages of diapers and wipes. "This is Charlotte. I think."

"Hey, Macey." Laramie inhaled the sweet scent of the baby's skin and tried to assess the situation.

"The social worker just left." Jack plucked a canister of formula from the box on the floor. "I was trying to figure out how to feed them and change their diapers." He stared at the label, his brows tented. "But I'm pretty much clueless when it comes to babies."

"Their social worker?" Laramie shifted Macey to her other shoulder and looked around for a place to change a diaper.

Jack blew out a long breath. "Breaking news, she said Macey and Charlotte are my daughters. Their mother—" He paused, his expression pained. "Their mother passed away and the State of Colorado says they need to be with their father, I'm not a felon, blah-blah-blah. Then she left, and here we are."

Thankfully, Laramie had cleared a spot on the end of the sofa, and sat down as Jack's words registered. Daughters. Jack was a father. Her shock and disbelief must've been written all over her face.

"Yeah, that was my reaction, too." Jack set the formula down and blew out a long breath. "I met their mother at a conference. She failed to mention she got pregnant after we spent the weekend together. I just found out she was killed in a car accident. So now the babies are going to live with me."

"Oh, Jack." Laramie's heart ached for him. "That's a lot to absorb in one day."

"My mom is going to be so disappointed. I've made horrible choices and she doesn't know the half of it."

Laramie found a waterproof pad in the pile of baby belongings and spread it beside her. Jack wasn't wrong. Mrs. Tomlinson and Jack's siblings had experienced a similar scenario recently when a relative left a baby boy in their care and skipped town. While Connor had been adopted by Skye and Gage eventually, the whole process was gut-wrenching. Finding out Jack was a father of two babies was going to be yet another blow to his family. Especially because his erratic behavior had been a source of worry and frustration ever since his father died three years ago.

She quickly changed Macey's diaper, which temporarily stopped the crying. But the baby girl shoved her fist in her mouth and started fussing again.

"She's hungry." Laramie glanced around the room. "Have you found bottles yet?"

"Right here." Jack held up two.

Charlotte spotted them and cried louder. She rolled over onto her tummy and dug her elbows into the carpet, as if by sheer determination she could crawl to Jack.

His eyes grew wide. "Please tell me she can't crawl yet."

"Looks like she's almost figured it out. You'd better let me fix the bottles." Laramie scooped Macey up, passed her to Jack, then took the bottles and formula into the kitchen.

When she returned a few minutes later with two warm bottles of formula, she handed one to Jack. "Here, you feed Macey while I change Charlotte."

Macey's eyes widened and she kicked her legs as Jack sat in the recliner and struggled to hold her and give her the bottle.

"Like this." Laramie leaned over, acutely aware of Jack's masculine, spicy scent and his breath feathering her cheek as she gently wedged Macey in the crook of his arm, then gave her the bottle. Macey quietly sucked down the formula while staring up at Jack, one pudgy hand grasping his finger.

Laramie's breath hitched at the innocent gesture. If Jack holding the puppy had pulled her in, this situation would be her undoing. But she couldn't bear to look at Jack and gauge his reaction. Not that she had time to stop and soak in the tender moment between father and daughter. Charlotte seemed determined that her sister wouldn't get all the attention. Her crying morphed into screaming.

"I'm coming." Laramie sat cross-legged on the floor and lifted the distraught baby into her arms. "Charlotte, listen, there's no need for all that crying."

Charlotte arched her back, grabbed a fistful of Laramie's shirt and cried louder. If that was even possible.

"All right, message delivered." Laramie changed Charlotte's diaper in record time and offered her the bottle. The baby gulped noisily, her tiny brow still furrowed, as she clung to the bottle with both hands. Good thing Laramie had spent all those years nannying to pay for college.

"See? That wasn't so bad." Laramie flashed Jack a smile from her place on the floor.

Her attempt at humor fell flat. His jaw flexed and his steely blue gaze was all business. "I need your help."

"I can only feed one baby at a time."

"Not just today. I mean, every day. Maybe every night, too. You took care of babies before."

Seriously? She felt sorry for Jack, and helping someone in need was always fulfilling, but lately she was saying yes to helping way too often. Besides, she'd listened to Skye vent plenty of times about Jack always shirking responsibility. "I'm not moving in and I'm not your nanny. I have a job, thank you."

"I thought school was out. Aren't you off all summer?"

"That doesn't mean I don't have plans." Maybe she didn't have plans *all summer*, but he didn't know that. These babies were *not* her problem.

"I know I don't have any right to ask you to upend your life, but at least for a few days until I can figure out what in the world I'm supposed to do."

"You can't keep twins a secret, Jack." Laramie couldn't stop the amusement from seeping into her voice. "Besides, just an hour ago at my house, you said you had a lot of attention to offer."

He shot her a pointed look. "Puppies and babies are hardly the same thing."

Jack shifted Macey in his arms and glanced back at Laramie. "Please. I need some time to figure out the best way to tell my family."

Those pleading blue eyes nailed her square in the heart. She wanted to say no. She should say no. But the babies were adorable, plus Jack obviously had no idea what he was doing.

"I'll help you get the babies settled and down for their naps, but you're on your own overnight. I'll be back in the morning, and you have to tell your family about the twins before the Memorial Day picnic." There. She'd established a boundary and a deadline. He had three days. That was the right thing to do, wasn't it?

Later, as she strode toward her car, she couldn't shake the ominous feeling blanketing her. What had she gotten herself into?

Chapter Two

In the history of worst nights ever, last night had to rank in his top five. Early-morning light peeked through the kitchen window as Jack stumbled toward the coffee maker. *Please let there be enough coffee to make a full pot.* He'd slept a grand total of two hours. Macey and Charlotte had conspired against him and taken turns crying off and on almost all night. Thankfully, they were both still asleep, but he didn't have the luxury of staying in bed. His most demanding client had scheduled an 8 a.m. video conference call, which meant he had to figure out how to shower, eat breakfast, change two diapers, feed the girls and, most important, keep them occupied while he took the call in his home office.

So basically, achieve the impossible. Awesome.

As soon as the coffee was brewing, he started a search for his phone. No telling where it had ended up.

He didn't want to pester Laramie about when she was coming back to help him, but he hoped it was soon. If he could just find his phone and see if she'd sent him a text yet. Having Laramie around would sure make the conference call easier. While the rest of the country was looking forward to Memorial Day weekend and making plans to celebrate, he had to keep his client happy. After all, cybersecurity criminals didn't slow down for a national holiday. Or the shocking revelation that he was a single father of two.

As he pulled a soggy dish towel and a men's fitness magazine off the granite counter cluttered with baby formula and used bottles, movement on the video monitor screen he'd unpacked from the box Miranda brought caught his eye.

One of the babies was awake and snuggled up next to her sister, babbling softly. He had to admit they were cute, even though they'd reduced him to a bumbling idiot. He'd hesitated putting them in the same portable crib to sleep, but Miranda's notes said they were used to sleeping together and he wasn't about to mess with their routine. The poor things had endured enough change already. Besides, his options were limited. There was no way he was calling Skye and Gage and asking to borrow a crib. The clock was ticking on Laramie's seventy-two-hour deadline to tell his family about the babies, and he needed every possible minute to come up with a viable plan.

Although he was exhausted and had little time to spare, he couldn't help but stare at the monitor. He wasn't sure if he was watching Charlotte or Macey, but she was adorable in her purple-polka-dotted pajamas as she made those innocent little cooing sounds. Jack forced himself to turn away and stay on task. He couldn't afford to waste precious minutes staring at the babies. His daughters. He still couldn't fully grasp the fact yet.

After flinging the towel in the general direction of

the laundry closet in the hallway, he went into the living room and pawed through the baby supplies scattered across the leather sofa. Normally he didn't mind a bit of disorganization and clutter, but this mess was over the top, even for him. His phone wasn't anywhere to be found.

Without warning, the sweet coos morphed into the alarming whimpers of impatient, hungry babies. The search for his phone would have to wait. So would coffee, breakfast and a shower, apparently. Man, he hoped Laramie showed up soon.

The stench that greeted him when he entered the small bedroom he'd put the crib in made him cough and cover his nose with the edge of his T-shirt.

"Oh my." Jack leaned over the frame of the portable crib and lifted Macey into his arms. "C'mon, let's get you cleaned up and ready for breakfast."

She didn't cry any louder as he tucked her against his shoulder and tried to do that bouncing-shushing move Laramie had done yesterday. He felt so foolish, and Macey didn't cry any less, either. Or was it that Charlotte was so much louder?

As Jack carefully lowered Macey to the changing pad he'd arranged on the floor, Charlotte rolled onto her side and ramped up the crying, her pale blue eyes churning out fat, pitiful tears.

"I'm sorry, sweet girl, I'm trying to hurry." Why were there so many snaps on the legs of these pajamas?

"Need some help?"

He glanced up to see Laramie standing in the bedroom doorway, wearing a pink V-neck T-shirt and denim shorts. She'd twisted her long blond hair into two braids, and Jack tried not to stare at her tan legs or the bright pink nail polish on her bare toes.

"Boy, am I glad to see you." Jack breathed a sigh. "I didn't even hear you come in."

Her green eyes gleamed with amusement. "It's a little loud and I'm sure you're distracted."

"True." Jack turned his attention back toward Macey. He'd made zero progress on the diaper situation and she was slurping noisily on her tiny fist.

Laramie sank to her knees beside him. "Why don't you go prep the bottles and I'll change their diapers."

He wanted to hug her. "Thank you. Seriously, you have no idea."

"Oh, I think I do." Laramie grinned at Macey. "Your daddy will be here all day trying to figure out how to clean you up, won't he?"

"Hey." Jack pretended to be annoyed. "I changed them both—twice—during the night."

Laramie's eyes widened. "No way."

Jack pushed to his feet. "But we didn't sleep much because it took me so long."

Laramie laughed and Jack hesitated, staring in amazement as she stopped Charlotte's crying with a small stuffed animal attached to a pacifier. He'd always liked her laugh. Spontaneous and unhindered. But what he really admired right now was her ability to soothe Charlotte.

"How did you do that?"

"Do what?"

"Get her to stop crying so easily?"

Laramie shrugged. "She seems to like the pacifier, and when it's clipped to a stuffed animal, it's more comforting, I guess."

She was a natural at caring for others, while he had to work so hard to even notice what another human needed. And now he had two babies living in his house with no end to their neediness. He was in way over his head.

"Have you thought about how you're going to tell your family you have twins?"

Laramie hadn't meant to go there quite so fast. *Real subtle, girl.* As they sat on opposite ends of Jack's leather sofa, each feeding a baby a bottle, she could tell by the tightness in his jaw that her question aggravated him.

"I'm taking this one minute at a time," he said, his eyes riveted on Macey, snuggled in the crook of his arm.

For a guy who hadn't known about his twins until yesterday, he was taking care of the babies with remarkably little complaining. Laramie had to give him a tiny bit of credit for that. Macey stared at him, then extended one chubby finger and explored his chin, which made Laramie's chest constrict.

Jack was already the kind of guy who drew the attention of every woman in the room when he made an entrance. Now, with his jeans, bare feet, a moss green T-shirt and that golden stubble clinging to his chin, he was making it difficult for Laramie to pay attention to Charlotte, who was almost finished with her bottle. If the world could only see Jack smiling at his baby girl and holding her as if she might break, every single woman from here to Kansas would be lined up outside his door.

The thought made Laramie's stomach tighten for a completely different reason. Not a protective, older-sister feeling, either. No. A jealous, territorial kind of reaction.

She mentally blocked the notion, just like she coached her volleyball players to block an opponent's attack. Jack was handsome and funny and spontaneous, but look what those qualities had led to. He'd had a fling with some girl in Vegas and now he was a father of two. Laramie wasn't a fan of that kind of dangerous spontaneity. These babies were his. As in forever. He couldn't just leave when life was hard and let somebody else take care of them, which was what she feared might happen. Jack was accustomed to letting other people deal with messes while he conveniently disappeared. And she refused to be the enabler. Not this time.

Charlotte pushed her bottle away, then grinned and cooed, demanding Laramie's attention.

"All done, cutie pie?" Laramie smiled and set the bottle aside, then carefully sat Charlotte upright and patted her on the back. "You are such a good girl."

Charlotte babbled in response, and Laramie couldn't help but laugh at the baby's timing. Her pudgy cheeks, long eyelashes and porcelain skin were irresistible, too.

"Have you figured out how to tell them apart?" Jack leaned forward and set Macey's empty bottle on the coffee table. "And how do I burp her again?"

Laramie demonstrated while she studied both babies for a trait or a detail that distinguished their identity. "They both have your blue eyes. It seems Macey has more hair than Charlotte, at least for now."

Macey leaned forward, intent on grabbing the remote control wedged in the sofa cushions. Her blond hair was thicker than her sister's and twisted into the beginnings of curls at the nape of her neck.

"I don't think so, little girl." Jack rescued the remote and set it on the dark wood-and-metal-framed coffee table. Macey's features crumpled and she started to wail.

"Oh no." Jack's eyes grew wide. "What do I do?"

Laramie couldn't help but chuckle. "Welcome to the rest of your life, dude. Kids don't like it when their parents say no. You might as well get used to it."

Macey cried louder, which somehow prompted Charlotte to join in. Laramie bounced her knee up and down, hoping motion might help.

"Seriously, Laramie." Jack raised his voice to be heard. "What do we do? I don't have time for this."

"Oh, and you think I do?" Laramie narrowed her gaze. "I don't have kids, Jack. I'm flying by the seat of my pants, too. By the way, I'm giving up time with my family and friends to help you out, so how about a little gratitude?"

Wow, okay. Where did that come from?

The expression on Jack's face indicated he was thinking the same thing. Heat warmed her skin as she stood, balanced Charlotte on her hip and dug through the supplies their social worker had brought. She'd packed plenty of clothes and a few blankets, but not a lot of toys. Finally, tucked under a pair of pajamas, Laramie found a book about animals with vinyl pages suitable for a baby to play with.

"Here." She handed it to Charlotte, who immediately stopped crying and put the corner of the book in her mouth. Laramie settled her on a blanket in front of Jack's leather recliner.

Macey, apparently still wounded over Jack's decision

to take the remote away, kept crying while Jack held her on his lap, paralyzed with indecision.

"Macey, look." Laramie found a stack of rainbow-colored plastic cups in the box with the clothes and blankets. "Want to play with these?"

Macey paused and drew a breath, giving Laramie the opportunity to pluck her from Jack's lap and put her next to her sister. Maybe that would buy them a few minutes' peace and give her time to come up with an explanation that justified her outburst.

"Laramie, I'm sorry." Jack's deep voice sounded genuinely contrite. "It was a long night and I wasn't thinking clearly. I never meant to imply that caring for babies was just for women. And I—"

"Don't worry about it." She pulled the clothes and blankets from the box and arranged them in neat stacks on the sofa. Creating order out of chaos always calmed her.

"I am worried. You're obviously upset and the last thing I want to do is offend you."

She forced herself to meet his gaze. The concern and regret swimming in those fathomless pools of blue softened her defenses. "It's okay. I know you're in shock and feeling overwhelmed. You need to find reliable childcare, Jack. As soon as possible."

"Got it." Jack held up both palms toward her. "A long-term solution is my first priority. And thank you for helping me. Helping us."

"You're welcome." Laramie quickly emptied the rest of the box. "Now where can I put these clothes and blankets?"

Jack palmed the back of his neck, still watching her, as if he had more to say but decided against it. "How about in the bedroom where the girls are sleeping? There's space in the dresser."

"Got it."

"Would you like some coffee?"

"Please," she called back over her shoulder as she strode from the room, a stack of blankets and baby clothes in her arms. Putting Macey and Charlotte's things away did little to erase her embarrassment. Her harsh words had surprised her. Jack, too. Even though she'd apologized, and he was quick to extend grace, she couldn't stand the feelings still nagging her. Instead of feeling proud of herself for giving Jack boundaries and a deadline, she felt melodramatic and confused. The fact that he looked devastatingly handsome holding his baby girls wasn't helping, either. She'd help him with Charlotte and Macey this weekend, but she wouldn't allow him to steal her heart.

While a husband and children were all she'd ever wanted, Jack and his twin daughters were not the answer to her prayers.

Jack ended the video conference call, then buried his head in his hands. It was only nine fifteen and he needed a third cup of coffee. Plus a whole lot of courage to tell Laramie he had to be on the next flight to Kansas City to address this security breach.

She was going to have a fit.

He'd tried telling the CEO that he was dealing with a family emergency, but that didn't fly because the CEO didn't have a family. As far as the man was concerned, a cybersecurity threat was the only acceptable kind of emergency. Maybe pouring himself into his career hadn't been the smartest move after all. He'd trained his clients to assume that he would always be available.

Dreading his conversation with Laramie, he pushed back his desk chair and crossed the guest room that doubled as a home office. In the kitchen, Laramie silenced him with a finger to her lips and a fierce glare.

Jack halted his steps and let his gaze sweep around the room, which was the cleanest he'd seen in a very long time. Quite possibly since the day he'd moved in.

"They're both napping," she whispered. Her unspoken message was crystal clear. *Don't mess this up.*

"That's amazing." He tiptoed past her to the coffee maker. "How did you manage that?"

"Pacifiers and the white noise app on my phone."

"Genius." Jack offered his palm and she slapped it with her own. "Thank you."

He poured a mug full of coffee, then angled his head toward the bare countertops. "You did not have to clean up my kitchen."

"Oh, but I did." She grimaced. "How can you live with so much…stuff everywhere?"

Jack lifted one shoulder. "Get used to it after a while."

"Gross."

He chuckled and stirred a generous helping of sugar into his coffee.

"How was your conference call?"

Stalling, he leaned against the counter and faced her, silently praying she'd see things from his perspective. "Not good. There was a huge data breach with my biggest client overnight. I need to leave for Kansas City, so I was wondering if—"

"Absolutely not."

"I haven't even asked yet."

"I already know what you're going to say, and the answer is no." She tipped her chin up, green eyes flashing with irritation. "I'm sorry to hear about the data breach, but you'll have to tell your client that you're not available."

"I tried that." Jack sipped his coffee, wincing as the liquid burned all the way down.

"Then tell him again."

"Please, Laramie. You're the only person I can ask to stay with the babies."

"That is so not true. Your mom, your brother, Skye and Gage are all less than ten minutes away."

"But I'd have to tell them about the twins and ask them to spend the night. That's not going to be a short conversation. Besides, they're strangers to the girls."

"And I'm not a stranger?" Laramie's brows arched. "I've spent less than five hours with them."

"That's five hours more than anyone else we know."

It was a weak argument and he knew it. Especially after their tense conversation earlier, when he'd accidentally implied his time was more valuable than hers. He really needed to convince Laramie she could do this, even if she claimed she wasn't the ideal person to rescue him. After all, she'd known exactly how to feed, change and soothe the twins, so he could get to work feeling confident Macey and Charlotte were in very capable hands.

"What about Trixie and her puppies? I can't leave them alone, either."

"Bring them here."

"That's crazy. You're going to add a goldendoodle and two puppies to this circus?"

A smile tugged at his mouth. "I love that you've diagnosed my life as a circus. It's an accurate description, by the way. And yes. What's not to love about Trixie and her puppies? You can set them up in my office."

"Jack, no." Laramie jammed her fists on her hips. "This isn't going to work. You'll have to come up with a plan B."

"That's the problem. There isn't a plan B. And I have to be in Denver by noon to make my flight. While I'd love to call my mother and let her know she's a grandmother of twin girls, this isn't the right time. If you'll bail me out, I promise I'll be back as soon as I can."

"Define as soon as you can." She quoted the air with her fingertips.

He set his coffee down and mentally calculated how long it would take him to assess the situation, then get a project manager in place. "I'll be back tomorrow night."

"Fine. On two conditions."

"Name them."

"You'll shop for groceries on your way home. Diapers, wipes, formula plus everything I need for the picnic on Monday. I've got pies to bake and I'm not showing up to my parents' house empty-handed because of you."

"Done and done." Before he realized what he was doing, he swept Laramie into a hug and pressed a kiss to the top of her head.

Man, she smelled good. And she fit nicely in his arms. Wait. What? His whole world slowed. Suddenly he wasn't in such a hurry to leave, and the hum of the dishwasher faded into the background, and all he could think about was why he hadn't hugged her sooner.

She eased out of his embrace and grabbed her car

keys off the counter. "I'll go get Trixie and her puppies and pack a bag."

"Sounds good." She avoided his gaze. The air in the room felt thick. Why had he hugged her, anyway? "I need a few minutes to get my stuff together anyway."

"I'll be right back." She strode toward the door and slipped out quietly.

Instead of getting ready to go, he cradled his mug in both hands and watched Laramie through the window above the kitchen sink. She was beautiful, kind and loving. He didn't get to see her feisty side very often and he kind of liked her spunk.

"Laramie Chambers, someday you are going to make a man very happy," he whispered and drained the last of his coffee.

Too bad that man wasn't him. She was organized, goal-oriented and devoted to her faith and family. He was impulsive and guilt-ridden, and having started running from his mistakes, had no idea how to stop now. Even today's visit to Kansas City was, in a way, an excuse to leave town and let Laramie take care of his children. She'd already refused to be the twins' permanent caregiver. And honestly, he couldn't blame her. Laramie was right. She shouldn't rearrange her whole life because he was having a crisis. He'd take this quick trip for work and then he'd come home and find a way to solve his own problems for once.

Chapter Three

Why had she let Jack talk her into this?

The clock on the oven in Jack's kitchen read 3:52 a.m. as Laramie slowly walked another lap around the island, then through the living room past Jack's sofa. Even Trixie was snoring on her bed in the living room, with both her puppies snuggled against her tummy. Laramie was beyond exhausted, and her arms and shoulders ached from holding Charlotte, but she woke up every time Laramie tried to put her in the portable crib beside Macey. Walking and humming softly seemed to be the secret to Charlotte's happiness, but Laramie wasn't sure how much longer she could keep this up. Especially since Macey would probably be awake soon, too.

All her confidence from the night before had vanished, and now she was counting the minutes until Jack got home. Maybe it was time to call for reinforcements as soon as the sun came up. Skye or Mrs. Tomlinson or even her own mother would all come to her rescue. That was one of the reasons she loved living in Merritt's Crossing. People genuinely cared for one another. Except lately she'd been so focused on what everybody else needed that she'd pushed her own dreams and plans aside. Again. Story of her life. Anyway, no matter how aggravated she was with Jack for getting himself into this mess, she'd promised she'd keep his secret until he got back from Kansas City later today. Caring for the babies by herself was a lot of work, but it wasn't her place to tell Jack's family about the twins, so she'd have to find a way to make it through the next several hours alone.

As she walked into the kitchen and rounded the island again, she glanced down at Charlotte asleep in her arms and admired the baby's long eyelashes, flawless skin and perfect cherubic mouth.

This is everything you've ever wanted.

The realization flitted through her mind and she tried quickly to dismiss it. Probably her lack of sleep making her think such irrational thoughts. Laramie carefully tucked Charlotte into the crook of her opposite arm and kept moving. She did want a husband, a house with a big yard and children of her own. And every minute she spent in Jack's house only made her more aware of everything she'd always liked about his place. From the leather furniture and hardwood floors to the impressive river-rock fireplace in the living room, it was way too easy to envision a future here with the babies. And Jack.

Except Jack had only called her because he needed reliable childcare. Worse, he was a master at dodging complicated situations. The twins were a perfect example of his inability to commit to anything other than his career and making sure life was one big continuous party. He'd conceived children after a one-night stand, and she couldn't remember the last time she'd seen him in church. This was not the kind of guy she wanted to trust with her heart. Her chest ached at the painful reminders of why Jack was so wrong for her.

She caught a glimpse of the framed photos on his bookshelf in the living room and stopped to study each one again. A picture of Jack hiking in Yosemite National Park, another with his college buddies at a professional baseball game and a third commemorating his whitewater rafting trip down the Colorado River all highlighted his independence and the many ways he'd tried to cope with the loss of his father and uncle.

Laramie shifted her gaze to the beautiful baby in her arms. Jack wasn't ready to be a father. No matter how precious the girls were, she refused to be the long-term solution to his latest crisis. Even her generosity had its limitations. Jack wasn't interested in a relationship with her. They'd known each other their whole lives. If he wanted to be more than friends, he would've asked by now.

Although it hurt to acknowledge the truth, she knew he'd only called her because she'd worked as a nanny before. Jack was just desperate. She should've told him no. Let him clean up his own mess. Why did she always say yes when someone needed her help? Regret and irritation mingled with fatigue and she stared longingly at the recliner nearby. If the babies were both asleep, maybe she could sneak in a quick nap, too.

Laramie eased into the leather chair, holding her breath as she slowly leaned back and willed Charlotte not to wake up. As soon as Jack came home, she'd hand off the babies, then spend the rest of the day baking pies and cookies for the Memorial Day celebration with her family. She'd make chocolate chip cookies. Her grandfather's favorite. Since she wasn't sure how many more family picnics she'd be able to celebrate with him, she wanted to bake something he really loved.

Her eyelids grew heavy and she finally relaxed, succumbing to the comfort of the chair and the warmth of Charlotte snuggled against her chest. If only she could get a little bit of rest, she'd have the energy to get through the morning until Jack came home.

She'd only been asleep a few minutes when Macey's cry filtered through the baby monitor.

Oh no.

"Please, not yet," she whispered into the darkness. She wasn't used to taking care of twins, especially when she hadn't had more than two hours of sleep. Macey kept crying, so Laramie forced herself to stand, hoping Charlotte wouldn't wake up, too. As she walked past the kitchen counter on her way to the babies' room, her phone lit up with an incoming text message.

She hesitated. Read the message or get to Macey right away? A predawn text message was probably important. She leaned closer. And it was from Jack. Hopefully he was letting her know he was taking an earlier flight.

Good morning. My flight was canceled due to bad weather. I'm trying to get on the next flight at three this afternoon. I'm so sorry. I've already called my brother and woke him up. He'll come by in a few hours with groceries and he can stay with the girls until I get home. Please text me when you wake up so I know you got this message.

Laramie wanted to scream. Of course Jack's flight was canceled. She should've known he wouldn't come home when he'd planned. While sending Drew over with diapers and formula was a good idea, she wasn't convinced he could handle taking care of the girls by himself. He was a great guy and all, but he didn't have kids. She'd only known him to babysit his nephew, Connor, a handful of times. Could she leave him alone for several hours with twin babies? And how would Charlotte and Macey react to yet another stranger?

As she padded into the babies' room, Charlotte's face crumpled with distress and she started to fuss. Macey's cries echoed louder, and Laramie blew out a long breath.

"Jack Tomlinson, you are in so much trouble."

When he finally did come home, Laramie was going to give him a piece of her mind. He should've canceled his trip to Kansas City and let someone else handle the data breach. There were other cybersecurity analysts available. As usual, when a crisis impacted his family, Jack had conveniently left town. Fatherhood was going to be a rude awakening for a guy who was accustomed to shirking his responsibilities. And she wasn't going to let him leave his daughters like this again.

On Sunday afternoon, Jack eased his truck into his driveway and turned off the ignition. He'd hoped to see Drew's truck parked by the garage, but Laramie's sedan was there instead. Drew had texted that he'd brought diapers and formula but hadn't stayed with the twins, like they'd discussed. Jack's scalp prickled. She was going to be so aggravated with him for coming home a day late. Just like everyone else in his life. He was used to disappointing people, but he hated disappointing Laramie. Getting stranded in Kansas City was a disaster, especially since she'd asked him not to go and he'd ignored her request.

Shouldering his backpack, he grabbed the two bags of groceries he'd picked up on the way home and exited the truck. His steps quickened at the thought of seeing Macey and Charlotte. Although he was still in shock that he was a father, he was pleasantly surprised how often he'd thought about the girls over the weekend.

Bracing for the anger and frustration he expected to see in Laramie's eyes, he quietly eased the door open. Silence greeted him. The comforting aroma of clean laundry and a hint of something delicious cooking in the kitchen enveloped Jack as he stepped inside. He set the groceries and his backpack down, then listened for the sound of babies crying or Laramie's voice. Trixie stood and trotted toward him, both her puppies scampering behind her.

"Hey, girl." Jack scratched her behind the ears. Tail wagging, Trixie leaned against his legs. At least she was happy to see him. "Where is everybody?"

He glanced toward the sofa in the living room and his breath caught at the sight of Laramie asleep in his recliner with one of the babies snuggled in her arms. The baby—he was pretty sure it was Charlotte—had her cheek pressed against Laramie's shoulder and her mouth was hanging open. Laramie's beautiful long blond hair spilled around her like a platinum pool and her manicured fingertips were braced protectively around Charlotte's backside. Her eyes were closed, allowing him to admire her peaceful expression. This whole scenario did a number on his heart, though. Seeing her asleep in his favorite chair and holding one of his daughters nearly took him to his knees.

He didn't deserve a friend like Laramie. His life was a mess, as usual, and she'd graciously stepped in and rescued him, like she often did when she realized her friends and family were struggling. And these precious girls needed two parents—not a mixed-up guy who only knew how to run from his problems. He'd heard what the social worker said about attachment and bonding and the twins needing their father, but he still had his doubts that he was the right person to have permanent custody.

Jack patted Trixie on the head, then tiptoed through the house and down the hall to the babies' room. Gently nudging the door open, he peeked inside. Macey was lying on her back in the portable crib, babbling quietly. She turned her head and met his gaze, then offered him a toothless grin through the mesh wall.

Jack's insides melted. "Hey, Macey."

She babbled louder and he crossed the room and scooped her up. "How's it going?"

Macey shoved her fist in her mouth, then squirmed in his arms. Was she hungry? Or was she hoping to see a familiar face? At least she wasn't screaming. Yet.

"Are you looking for your sister?" Jack clumsily sank to the floor where Laramie had arranged another package of diapers and a container of wipes. He was still lousy at changing diapers, but he figured it out. Thankfully, Macey's green-and-white-striped outfit had a zipper this time.

Lifting Macey into his arms, he carefully tossed the diaper into the trash, still feeling a little awkward carrying a baby. As soon as he walked down the hallway and into the living room, she saw Laramie and Charlotte asleep in the recliner and squealed with excitement.

"Shhh," he said, chuckling softly at her reaction.

Laramie's eyes fluttered open, then widened as she recognized Jack. "You're home."

"Hey."

"What time is it?" She glanced down at Charlotte asleep in her arms.

"Almost four." He winced. "I'm sorry."

She met his gaze again, her green eyes narrowed. "For what?"

"For being late, making you stay with the girls, Drew leaving." He shifted from one foot to the other, trying to appease Macey as she squirmed and fussed.

"You're here now. That's what matters." Laramie pushed to her feet, then tucked Charlotte into the crook of her arm. Macey kicked her leg against Jack's hip as Laramie moved closer.

Laramie's brow furrowed. "What's wrong, pumpkin?"

Macey leaned away from Jack with both of her arms outstretched.

"She wants you," he said.

"Can you hold Charlotte?" Laramie passed him the sleeping baby without waiting for his response. "We can trade."

"Right." Their fingers brushed as he scooped Charlotte into his arms and tried to focus on keeping her asleep so he wasn't distracted by the warmth of Laramie's touch or her ability to soothe Macey's crying instantly. His daughters needed Laramie. *He* needed Laramie. So how could he convince her to stay?

Laramie turned away and moved toward the oven, singing softly to Macey. The baby's chubby hand grasped a fistful of Laramie's yellow T-shirt. Jack stole a quick glance at Laramie's white shorts and tan legs. Even though she'd spent the weekend caring for two babies, and probably hadn't had more than a few minutes to herself, she was as beautiful as ever.

"Where's Drew?"

She lifted the lid on the saucepan and peeked inside. "I sent him home."

"Why?"

Laramie shot him a pointed look over her shoulder. "Your brother's a great guy, but he cannot handle twins by himself."

Jack scrubbed his palm over his face. "He didn't help you at all?"

"He stayed for a few hours, then I sent him home." Laramie stirred whatever was simmering in the pan and put the lid back. "He had to work today anyway."

Jack glanced from Macey wedged on Laramie's hip to Charlotte cradled against his chest. His stomach coiled in a knot. He couldn't handle twins, either. He had to ask Laramie to keep helping him. What was he going to do if she said no?

"What did your mom say when you told her about the twins?"

Jack hesitated. "I didn't tell her yet."

"Jack." She glared at him. "We had a deal."

"I know." He looked away, heat flooding his cheeks. He felt about ten years old, getting a lecture for yet another one of his lousy decisions.

She studied him. "What are you going to do about childcare?"

"That's what I need to talk to you about."

"I knew this was going to happen." Her mouth flattened. "The answer's no."

"Please, Laramie. You're so good for the girls and they're happy with you."

She started emptying the dishwasher with one hand and refused to look at him.

"Say something."

"You can't possibly know if the babies are happy, because you've barely spent any time with them."

Her voice carried an edge he hadn't heard very often. Almost like she was judging him. Not that he blamed her. He'd messed up big time. Didn't he get any credit for trying to do what was best for Macey and Charlotte, though? Laramie was exactly what they needed.

"Just until you start volleyball season in August."

"That's two months." Her expression was a mixture of worry and confusion. "I'm taking my volleyball team to camp in Fort Collins in July, and my family needs me, too."

"I'll figure out a way for you to help your family and watch the babies."

"Wow, thank you so much. Because taking care of people was exactly how I wanted to spend my entire summer break."

He winced. "I'm sorry. That didn't come out right. What I meant was I'll find someone to help part-time so you're not giving up your whole summer for us. And it might not even be until August. I'm applying for a job in Utah, so if that works out, then I'll only need your help until I move."

Laramie stilled, a dish halfway to the stack inside the cabinet. She turned slowly to face him, something unreadable flickering in her eyes.

He hadn't planned on telling her about the job in Utah until he had an interview lined up. Except he was tired of keeping secrets. Why was she staring at him like that? Shouldn't she be happy that he might not need her help for the whole summer?

"You're going to move out of state with two babies and a puppy?"

"It's a government job with great benefits and more stability."

"But you won't know anyone. The babies will have yet another new babysitter, plus a whole new house to get used to. If you have trouble, who will you call? You need your family now more than ever."

That was the problem. He didn't want to be near his family anymore. Charlotte's eyes opened and she started to cry, keeping him from blurting the words on the tip of his tongue. Jack appreciated her concern, but the twins were only six months old. If they were with him, what difference did it make if they lived here or in Utah? Besides, he couldn't stay in Merritt's Crossing any longer. The family's scandal surrounding Dad and Uncle Kenny's longstanding feud still haunted him. He knew his mom and his siblings wished he hadn't fought with his dad the day that he died. The blame weighed heavy. If he'd been more involved, maybe they'd both still be alive.

"I need a fresh start," he said. "Small towns have long memories and I'm tired of bumping into all the reminders of my failures."

She stared at him, her jaw tight. Then she extracted some of her hair from Macey's grasp. "I'll take care of the girls until July 15. Or until you move, but you have to tell your family about the babies by tomorrow."

"Thank you." Jack smiled and breathed a sigh, but he couldn't ignore the tension blanketing the space between them. The job in Utah might be a wonderful opportunity and a fresh start, but it meant saying goodbye to Laramie. He wasn't sure his heart could handle that, but it was best for everyone.

Chapter Four

Jack wanted to move to Utah.

His news had rolled into Laramie's world like a storm
blowing across the Front Range. She'd spent the rest of
the holiday weekend running his crazy plan through
her head and she still couldn't believe he was serious.

She squeezed the life out of her car's steering wheel
as she followed Jack's pickup truck into the modest sub-
division in Merritt's Crossing where his mother lived.

This morning's disastrous outing to the pediatrician
had underscored her concerns. He couldn't even take
the twins to the doctor without help. How was he going
to move to another state?

She parked in front of the Tomlinsons' house,
grabbed her purse and climbed out.

Jack took his time exiting his truck. The slump of
his shoulders and dark circles under his eyes hinted at
the kind of night he'd had.

She met him in the driveway and planted her hands
on her hips. "Does your mother know we're coming?"

Jack nodded, a muscle in his jaw twitching as he

opened the back door and reached in to unlatch Macey's car seat.

Does your mother know I'm *coming?* That was what she wanted to ask, but she resisted the urge to pepper him with questions. She'd planned to run errands while Jack introduced the twins to their grandmother. Until she'd witnessed his struggle getting the twins in and out of the truck, then stayed with him while they all endured their first visit with their new pediatrician. The doctor and her staff were excellent. Laramie and Jack were the problem—they had no idea how to cope with two fussy babies in an enclosed space.

Jack's pleading gaze and the look of sheer defeat on his face was all it took to convince her to meet him at his mom's place. Was she really that easily swayed? One pathetic glance from those incredible blue eyes and she completely blew off her plans? The realization nipped at her, like one of Trixie's puppies nipping at her fingers. But her errands could wait. The babies needed her. Besides, she'd already agreed to help him.

She circled around to the opposite side of his truck and maneuvered Charlotte's car seat from its base. The baby rewarded her with a smile that made Laramie's heart expand. Jack's girls were adorable. At least he had that working in his favor.

"What did your mom say when you told her about the twins?"

Jack shouldered the diaper bag and strode up the driveway with Macey's car seat in his hand. He didn't answer her.

Oh no. "Jack? You told her about Charlotte and Macey, right?"

He kept walking, the car seat bumping against his

leg. "Becoming a father like this isn't something I can tell her about over the phone."

Laramie glared at his back. Was he joking? "So she's going to find out right now?"

"Yep."

Laramie followed him up the steps while her stomach coiled in a tight knot. Poor Mrs. Tomlinson. Laramie wanted to jump in front of Jack and beg him to let her go in alone and prep his mom somehow. She was a strong woman, but news like this was a lot to absorb. Before Laramie could say a word, the front door opened, and Mrs. Tomlinson greeted them.

"Hi, sweetie." Her smile faltered as her gaze slid from Jack to the car seats and then to Laramie.

"Hi, Laramie."

She wished she could vanish into the porch. This was so awkward. All she could manage was a pathetic wave.

Mrs. Tomlinson's eyes toggled between the babies in the car seats. "Jack, what's going on?"

"Mom, I'd like you to meet my daughters, Macey and Charlotte."

"Your what?" Her complexion paled and her fingers trembled as she pressed her palms to her cheeks.

"It's a complicated story." Jack cleared his throat. "Can we come in? The babies need to eat."

Laramie snuck a glance at Jack, then winced at the pain etched on his face. *Please, please let us in.* She silently willed Mrs. Tomlinson to see past her own heartache and confusion and let them inside. Not just because it was time for the girls to drink their bottles, but because she also knew Jack needed his mother to hear him out. In his heart, he wanted to do what was right and hated to disappoint his family any more than he already had.

"Come on in." Mrs. Tomlinson stepped back and opened the door wider.

Thank You, Lord. Laramie silently offered the brief prayer as she trailed Jack inside. Mrs. Tomlinson swiped at the tears dampening her cheeks. Laramie's throat ached and she gave Mrs. Tomlinson's forearm a gentle squeeze. Although they'd all weathered the unexpected storm of baby Connor's mother abandoning him and celebrated when he found a permanent home with Skye and Gage, this was a much different scenario.

The aroma of an apple pie baking in the oven enveloped them and Laramie set the car seat in front of the familiar sofa where she'd spent countless hours over the years.

"I'll make the bottles." She stretched out her hand to take the diaper bag from Jack.

"No, that's okay. You don't—"

Laramie shot him a pointed look. "You and your mom need to…catch up. I'll change their diapers and get the bottles ready."

Jack relented and surrendered the diaper bag.

The modest rambler didn't offer too many places for her to go where she couldn't overhear their conversation, but she was determined to give Jack and his mom a few minutes alone.

While she mixed the formula in the bottles in Mrs. Tomlinson's kitchen, she glanced out the window at the backyard where the family often gathered. As Skye's best friend, Laramie had spent plenty of time in that yard. Now her imagination quickly sprinted ahead and offered images of her and Jack here together with the girls. Preschool-sized versions of Charlotte and Macey squabbling over who had the next turn on the rope swing suspended from the tree in the far corner. Laramie and Jack sitting in the chairs circled around the patio, while Gage or Drew grilled hamburgers and hot dogs for the whole family and the girls chased each other across the grassy lawn.

Stop being ridiculous. Disappointment snuffed out the happy thoughts and she quickly turned away from the window. Jack wasn't interested in her romantically. He only cared about the utilitarian role she played right now. She was foolish to get her hopes up that his feelings might change just because she knew how to change diapers and fix bottles. He even planned to move away as soon as he could. The only thing Jack wanted was a nanny.

This was hard. A million times harder than confessing he'd shoplifted the candy bar from the grocery store in town when he was eight. Harder than sneaking in past curfew his senior year and finding his mother waiting for him in that same chair. Harder than carrying his uncle and his father's caskets at their funerals.

His mother's tears wrecked him.

He should've listened to Laramie and told his mom about the twins before today.

Jack rubbed his clammy palms against the fabric of his cargo shorts and forced himself to meet his mother's troubled gaze.

"I never meant for this to happen." He winced, realizing how many times those same stupid words had left his lips. "The truth is, I was only thinking of myself. This is just another disappointment in a long string of mistakes and poor choices I've made. I'm sorry and I'm going to do what's right."

"Oh, Jack." Her expression crumpled and she reached for another tissue from the box on the coffee table between them.

Laramie strode into the room with Macey wedged on her hip and a warm bottle in her other hand. Macey was puffing out little gasps, reaching for the bottle with both hands and kicking her chubby leg against Laramie's hip.

"Hold on, sweet girl." Laramie stopped next to the coffee table, uncertainty flashing in her eyes as her gaze swung between him and his mother. "Sorry to interrupt, but I've got a hungry baby here. I still need to change Charlotte, too. Mrs. T., would you like to feed Macey?"

"Oh, I don't know if—"

Laramie silenced the protest by depositing Macey in Jack's mom's lap. "Here you go. I'll bring you a burp cloth in a minute."

Jack smothered a smile with his hand. He was beyond grateful for Laramie. This whole day would've been a disaster if he'd tried to fly solo. As she lifted a fussy Charlotte from her car seat and carried her out of the room, Jack couldn't help but stare after her. Taking care of people came as naturally as breathing for Laramie. Especially his girls. How was he ever going to find someone trustworthy, someone so attentive, when he moved?

"How long is Laramie helping you?"

Jack didn't miss the unspoken message underlying his mother's question. She knew he needed a truckload of help. But did she also suspect his feelings toward Laramie were changing? He'd need to keep that a secret, too. Although staring after her all doe-eyed was a great way to blow his cover.

"She's agreed to help me until she takes her team to volleyball camp. That starts July 15."

"Wow, that's very generous." His mom gently cradled Macey and tilted the bottle for her. Macey stared up at her grandmother, both hands gripping the plastic bottle while she drank noisily. She didn't seem to care who was holding her, as long as there was food involved.

"You know, Laramie's grandparents are struggling. You need to make sure she has plenty of time to take care of her own family, too."

Jack frowned. She had mentioned something about her grandparents. The last several days had been a blur, but snippets of their conversation from when he'd gone to visit the puppies at her house replayed in his mind.

"Yeah, of course. She can take whatever time she needs." He rubbed his fingertips along his stubbly jaw. Guilt pinched at his insides. Those words didn't exactly line up with how he'd behaved. He said she could do what she needed to do, but in reality, he'd monopolized all her free time. And hadn't bothered to pay attention to what really mattered most in her world—her family. Man, he was a real idiot sometimes. Maybe most of the time.

He'd have to do better. He *would* do better. Starting today.

Laramie came back into the room, Charlotte's cries echoing through the small house.

"Here, why don't you let me feed her and you can go on home?"

Confusion flashed in Laramie's eyes as she sat beside him on the sofa and offered Charlotte her bottle. "What? Why?"

"You've helped me a lot. Probably way too much. Don't you have things you want to do?"

Laramie's gaze swiveled toward his mom, then back to him. "Well, yeah, but I said I'd help you and—"

"I've got this." He held out his arms and Laramie hesitated before handing Charlotte over. He caught a familiar trace of Laramie's sweet floral perfume as she stood. Charlotte squirmed in his arms and he instantly regretted offering to take care of the girls on his own.

Laramie cast him one last doubtful look. "If you're sure…"

"Perfectly sure." Sort of. He forced a confident smile while Charlotte cried and pushed the bottle away.

"Nice to see you again, Mrs. Tomlinson," Laramie said, one hand on the doorknob as she glanced at Jack again. "Call me if you change your mind."

"I won't." Jack tilted his head toward the door. "Go on."

"I'll see you first thing in the morning."

Jack nodded, resisting the temptation to tell her he'd already changed his mind. After the door closed behind her, he sagged against the sofa cushions and blew out a long breath. Charlotte stared up at him, pitiful tears trailing down her pink cheeks.

"See? That wasn't so hard, was it?" his mother asked.

Jack frowned at her amused expression. "It's going to be another long night."

Mom chuckled. "I think you're right about that. And I hate to kick you while you're down, but I'm not going to be able to help you, either. I've got a date."

It's a good thing he was sitting down. "A what?"

"A date." Mom's expression glowed. "I met a nice man from Denver and he's taking me out for dinner tonight."

A *date*? A sour taste coated the back of Jack's throat. Did Skye and Drew know? Was Jack supposed to meet this guy?

"Good for you." Jack kept his focus on Charlotte, who'd settled down and changed her mind about drinking her bottle. He didn't want to hurt his mom's feelings, but he so wasn't ready to think about his mom seeing someone romantically.

"I guess we both had surprising news to share, didn't we?"

"I'm definitely surprised." Jack's words fell flat. He wanted to be happy for her. Really, he did. Even though three years had passed, he still wasn't over his father's death. Her news was another reminder of all they'd lost. Would he ever outrun the heartache?

"Grandma? Grandpa?" Laramie let herself into her grandparents' farmhouse and closed the door. "It's me."

The television blared from the family room toward the back of the house and the scuffed floorboards creaked under her sandals as she strode from the front hall into the kitchen.

"Hi, sweetie." Grandma stood at the yellow Formica counter, wearing a blue gingham blouse, white shorts and white sandals. Her silver hair was twisted into her trademark bun and she'd even put on a little bit of makeup, but the worry lingering in her gaze and her rounded shoulders confirmed Laramie's worst fears. Caring for Grandpa was wearing her grandmother out.

"Hi, Grandma." Laramie pressed a quick kiss to her soft cheek. "You look nice."

"Thank you." Grandma shrugged self-consciously. "It's just the gals I quilt with, but I felt like wearing lip gloss and a new blouse."

"Good for you." Laramie smiled. "I'm glad you can get together with your friends tonight."

"Me, too." Her smile wobbled. "I don't get to quilt too much anymore."

Laramie's heart ached for all her grandmother had given up to care for Grandpa. After decades of hard work and running the family farm they'd inherited, it was a shame her grandparents had to wrestle with Grandpa's dementia now that they finally had retired from farming.

Grandma tucked her wallet inside her purse, then hoisted her tote bag onto her shoulder. "Thank you for staying with your grandfather. I was so tickled when you called and offered."

"You're welcome." Laramie patted her arm. "Don't worry about a thing. Grandpa and I will be just fine."

"I know you will." Grandma hummed softly as she picked up a disposable container full of cookies. "He gets anxious when I leave, so I'm going to sneak out without saying goodbye."

Oh. Laramie's stomach tightened. What exactly did she mean by anxious? "Um, all right. Have fun."

"I'll be home by nine," Grandma whispered and slipped out the back door.

Laramie quickly scanned the counter for any notes or instructions. The dishwasher was running already. Knowing Grandma, she'd already fed Grandpa and cleaned up before Laramie arrived. She hadn't planned on spending the evening here, but her mother had asked her to because she knew how much Grandma wanted to go to her quilting group.

Besides, helping her grandparents tonight kept her from hopping back in her car and driving straight to Jack's place. Macey and Charlotte had occupied so much of her time and attention lately. She felt strange not being with them.

Oh, brother. She'd have to get over that, because leaving Jack and the twins alone for the evening was best for all of them. At least that was what she kept telling herself. Jack was a single dad now. He needed to get used to being responsible for the girls on his own.

Since dinner was taken care of and Grandma had managed to leave without Grandpa noticing, Laramie joined him in the family room. He sat in his faded green recliner, wearing his favorite Colorado Rockies T-shirt, black shorts and slippers.

Laramie's steps faltered when she saw the angry bull bucking his rider into the dirt on television. Great. The last thing she wanted was to watch bull riding, but if he got anxious when her grandmother was away, there was no reason to challenge his entertainment choices.

"Hey, Grandpa." Laramie sank to the floor beside his chair and patted his forearm. "What are you watching?"

His head swiveled slowly and his green eyes, which used to gleam like he'd just finished laughing at a good joke, narrowed into an icy, suspicious glare.

"Who are you?"

His harsh tone stung. "Grandpa, it's me. Laramie."

His leathery features puckered. "Like the town in Wyoming?"

She managed a nod, her throat thick with emotion.

He knew the whole story about how her parents met and promised to name their firstborn after the town where they'd fallen in love. Grandpa had heard it dozens of times. How could he not remember? And how could he not remember *her*?

"Huh." He grunted. "Don't reckon I know anyone named Laramie."

He pointed a gnarled finger toward the television. "I'm watching my grandson. He's a world champion bull rider. Ever heard of him?"

Laramie gritted her teeth and forced herself to look. Oh, yes. She knew her brother well. How he traveled the country, winning almost every competition he entered. Landon Chambers was the pride of Merritt's Crossing. How ironic that Grandpa had no trouble recognizing her brother, even though she couldn't recall the last time Landon had bothered to grace them with his presence. Even her aunt, uncle and cousins in Nebraska managed to get away from their busy lives on their own farm to visit a few times a year.

Thankfully, Grandpa didn't seem too concerned if she answered his question about Landon. Another bull rider entered the chute, preparing for the gate to open, and Landon wasn't slated to ride for a few more minutes.

She stood and pulled her phone from her shorts pocket. Her fingers pecked out a text message to Jack, but she hesitated before sending it. What was she doing? Checking up on him? Making sure he could handle an evening alone with his daughters? Laramie erased the message and put her phone away.

Instead of sitting in her grandmother's recliner beside Grandpa's and watching a competition she didn't care about, she crossed the small room and surveyed the framed photos filling the wall. Her grandparents' wedding portrait hung in the center, with dozens of other photos fanning out in opposite directions. Birthdays, graduations and harvest celebrations all documented a life well lived. Laramie's eyes burned with unshed tears. Dementia was a cruel robber, snatching away bits and pieces of the grandfather she'd always known and loved. She had to find a way to help him get the care he needed, before Grandma endangered her own health, too.

Chapter Five

"How long are you planning on scrubbing that pot?"
Jack cradled his coffee mug with both hands and leaned
against his kitchen counter. Laramie ignored him and
kept working at the oatmeal he was pretty sure had long
since disappeared. If she didn't stop, there wouldn't be
any enamel left on the inside.

She rinsed the pot off, then set it in the drying rack.
Before she reached for more of his dirty dishes, he put
his coffee down and turned off the water spigot.

"Hey." He dipped his head and forced her to meet his
gaze. "Thank you for helping me, but you don't need
to wash my dishes."

"Okay." She lifted a shoulder in a dismissive shrug
and turned away, drying her hands on a towel hanging
from the handle of the dishwasher.

Ouch. Talk about frigid. Laramie hadn't smiled since
she arrived an hour ago. What had he done? Jack mentally rehashed the last twenty-four hours. He'd taken
the twins to meet his mother, like Laramie thought he
should. Then he'd given her the rest of the day off and
hadn't called or texted her at all last night. Even though

he'd wanted to. Charlotte and Macey took forever to fall asleep and he'd been super frustrated, but he'd handled it all by himself.

Despite her evening away from him, this morning she was moody. Sullen. And currently extracting revenge on his kitchen counter. She scraped at a mysterious substance with her fingernail, then doused it with the spray bottle of vinegar and water, then attacked again with a fierce swipe of a paper towel.

Jack leaned against the opposite counter and reached for his coffee, unable to stop the laughter that bubbled up.

Laramie glared at him over her shoulder. "What's so funny?"

"You, trying to annihilate every speck of dirt from my kitchen. Breaking news—twins live here now. You'll never get ahead."

Boy, that was the wrong thing to say. Her eyes narrowed. She looked mad enough to spit fire.

She turned around and finished wiping the counter. A second later, he recognized the unmistakable sounds of a woman crying.

Oh no. No, no, no. Adrenaline hummed in his veins, but he couldn't move. He really, really hated it when Laramie cried. Her pain paralyzed him. She leaned both hands against the counter, her shoulders quaking as her crying grew louder.

Don't just stand here. Do something, dummy!

Jack abandoned his coffee again and crossed the small space in two long strides. "I'm sorry I laughed." He gently cupped her shoulder with his hand. "Please tell me what's wrong."

She buried her face in her hands and the tears kept coming.

His aversion to her pain was overcome by his desperate need to comfort her. He pulled her into his arms. "Whatever it is, I'm sure we can figure something out."

Jack pressed his cheek against the top of Laramie's head and gently stroked her long hair. She sobbed into his T-shirt, her body trembling, while her hands found their way to the small of his back. As she twisted her fists in the fabric of his shirt, Jack's pulse sped.

The fragrance of her shampoo and the warmth of her body against his sent his mind careening down a dangerous path.

You're friends, remember? She's helping care for your children.

He mentally squashed the notion of tipping her chin up and kissing those full, pink lips.

"M-my grandfather d-d-didn't recognize me yesterday."

Jack closed his eyes. She'd stuttered and her words were muffled, but he understood, and worse, recognized what Laramie had left unspoken. Grandpa Lyons was fighting a losing battle with dementia.

"I'm so sorry," he said. "That's awful."

"My brother was competing on TV and Grandpa knew exactly who he was."

Ouch. Landon had always been a big deal around Merritt's Crossing, even more so since he'd started winning all those bull-riding competitions. Jack knew a thing or two about living in the shadow of a sibling who could do no wrong. Skye had always been a conscientious overachiever.

"Your grandparents love you," he reminded her. "They're so proud of you and everything you've done for your students and the volleyball program."

She pulled away, swiping at her tears with her fingertips. "I have to do more to help my grandfather."

"Staying with him last night was probably a huge help."

The words had barely left his mouth and she was already shaking her head.

"No, I mean something big. Something significant. Jack, you should've seen my grandmother—she tried to cover it up with lip gloss and a new blouse, but she's exhausted. Caring for him is putting her own health at risk."

His chest ached. Laramie's grandmother was one of the sweetest women he'd ever known. The thought of her falling or getting sick and not being able to care for her husband was scary. No wonder Laramie was so upset.

"Have you considered calling your brother and asking him to help?" Jack almost put up his hands to block whatever she was probably going to throw at him for mentioning her brother.

"Ha." She barked out a laugh. "He has zero interest in helping figure this out. Besides, he invests all his earnings in a cattle ranch in Oklahoma."

Jack had heard Landon had reinvested some of his earnings but couldn't imagine he wouldn't be able to help with his grandfather's care, too. The guy had done well on the professional bull-riding circuit. Still, this wasn't the time to push Laramie. She was already shooting down all his suggestions.

"Breeding dogs was supposed to make more money." She huffed out a breath and snatched a tissue from the box on the counter. "Obviously that was a stupid plan."

"You can charge me double for mine."

Laramie flashed a wobbly smile. "That's sweet of you to say. I'm not charging you double, though."

"Then I can pay you more for taking care of the girls." He didn't even bother to mentally calculate what a raise might cost. "You've definitely earned a raise."

"No, stop." Her brow furrowed. "This isn't your problem to solve."

Oh, but he wanted to solve her problems. The thought blindsided him, just like his longing to kiss her a few minutes before. He wasn't going to be able to keep his feelings for her bottled up much longer.

Maybe pursuing that new job in Utah was the right decision after all. Time and distance would make him come to his senses. Once he moved and started over, he'd finally stop wanting Laramie.

She was a wreck. A soggy, emotional wreck. How embarrassing. Laramie tossed her crumpled tissue in the trash and avoided Jack's gaze. Why had she fallen into his arms? One minute she was cleaning up the kitchen, trying to ignore the spicy scent of his aftershave, and the next she was blubbering like an idiot and leaving a trail of tears on his blue T-shirt.

She didn't want to need him. She *refused* to need him. Because needing and wanting were dangerously intertwined. And he'd already decided he was moving. While his offer to pay her more money came from a good place, his so-called solutions just made her more upset.

"You and your family mean so much to this whole community." Jack's gentle tone and kind words did little to soothe her. The people of Merritt's Crossing had conquered a lot of obstacles over the years. Dementia was proving to be a formidable beast, though. A church committee, a cake walk at the county fair, a special offering at Sunday's service—none of the usual weapons in their arsenal would help this time. More tears pricked behind her eyes.

She would not fall apart again in front of Jack. Because he'd pull her against that broad, firm chest of his and whisper in her ear while he stroked her hair, and frankly, she didn't have the strength to push him away a second time.

She had to get away from his empathetic gaze and those strong arms. Oh, those arms. Laramie cast a pleading glance toward the baby monitor, wishing the twins would wake early from their morning nap. Sure, that would make for a miserable day, but at least she'd have something to distract her from thinking about how good it felt when Jack held her.

"If people know your grandparents are struggling, then they can help."

Jack followed her toward the washing machine in the hallway. She ignored him and tugged the clean clothes from the dryer and dropped them in the empty basket waiting on the floor.

"Why don't you call some of the ladies at church and ask them to arrange a team of volunteers? Then your grandmother can—"

"No." Laramie slammed the dryer closed. "My grandmother would be mortified, especially since wheat harvest starts soon. She knows how busy everyone gets. She doesn't want to be a burden."

Laramie grabbed the laundry and tried to carry it toward the living room.

Jack gently grasped both sides of the basket, blocking her from moving past him.

What was he doing? Didn't he have enough problems of his own to worry about?

"Laramie." His tender gaze searched her face. "Please let me help you. That's what friends are for."

Ah, friends. The dreaded label that meant their relationship was a dead end. The tears pressed in, threatening to spill over. See? This was exactly why she'd vowed not to need him. Because he'd never see her as anything more than what they were right now. Why did every single situation in her life have to circle back to her stupid feelings for Jack?

"Don't you get it?" she whispered. "There's nothing you can do. This disease is going to take my grandfather down. My parents will never sell the farm. And unless they can find someone to lease some of our land, or I figure out how to breed a dozen litters of puppies, none of us have enough money to get him into a care facility that will keep him safe."

Jack's eyes widened.

Anger, sadness and frustration churned into a nasty concoction and she couldn't stop the snide words from tumbling out.

"I'm afraid this is one of those times where you can't charm or sweet-talk your way to an easy solution. Now please move so I can fold this laundry."

Hurt flickered across his face. Silence filled the tiny laundry nook. Blood pounded behind her ears as her words echoed in her head. Okay, that was probably a little harsh. She refused to apologize, though. This time Jack couldn't tease away her troubles with a joke, or pelt her with snowballs, or give her the slice of birthday cake with the most frosting. All those remedies had worked when they were kids. When he was Skye's brother and she was his older sister's best friend and a steady constant at the Tomlinsons' house.

His phone chimed in his pocket. "I have to take this call."

Jack finally broke eye contact and turned away.

She watched him walk into his office at the end of the hall, then quietly close the door without looking back. That man was so confusing. He made her want to scream. If he cared about her, why was she still just his nanny and friend? Worse, why did he want to move away?

Jack ended the call and set his phone on his desk, then slumped back in his chair. He'd scheduled his first phone interview next week for the position in Utah. A hollow ache lodged in his chest, followed quickly by a mental image of Laramie swiping at her tear-stained face.

His chair squeaked as he dragged his palm down his cheek. Change was what he wanted.

Right?

The appeal of a new start and distance from the same old small-town life that was slowly suffocating him had motivated him to apply for the job. And how could he pass up excellent benefits and no more traveling? Especially since he was a father of two now.

Because Utah didn't include Laramie.

Macey and Charlotte were getting attached to her. He didn't know much about babies, but he could see the way they looked for Laramie when he carried them into a room. Jack empathized with their disappointment when they didn't see her. After she went home in the evenings, he counted the hours until she came back the next day.

Dude. You're pathetic. Tell her how you feel.

"It's not that simple," he growled, lacing his hands behind his head as he stared at the ceiling. Now that he knew how much her grandparents struggled with health issues he couldn't ask her to leave her family. She was so stubborn. She'd never agree to go with him, anyway.

Unless he found a solution to her grandparents' needs.

Jack leaned forward and grabbed his phone. Why hadn't he thought of this before? Adrenaline pulsed through his veins as he scrolled to Landon Chambers's number. He and Landon had grown up together, although Landon was a year behind Jack in school. They weren't best buddies or anything, but he and Landon had spent countless hours working on the farm, playing tag and hide-and-seek and finding new ways to aggravate Skye and Laramie. It wouldn't hurt to reach out to Landon and see when he was planning to come home for a visit.

This is one of those times you can't charm or sweet-talk your way into a solution.

Laramie's words replayed in his mind. Man, he didn't like that one bit. Since when had he charmed or sweet-talked his way out of anything? He stopped scrolling and glanced out the window. A cloudless blue sky and his neighbors' wheat fields dancing in the midday sunshine framed the woodshop hugging his property line. The same building Jack refused to enter. His stomach clenched. He'd learned a lot living in a farming community—working hard to achieve a goal, battling unknown obstacles like drought and hailstorms, celebrating an abundant harvest.

Building furniture was a lot like farming, and Jack's father and uncle had tried to teach him to turn pieces of wood into furniture, but Jack had lost interest. Especially when that same craft had led to his uncle's suicide, created a festering rift in their family and derailed his cousin McKenna's life. Not to mention the gossip that still circulated about his family and the curious looks that followed him whenever he went to Angie's Diner or Pizza, Etc. While a small part of Jack itched to build furniture again, he'd squelched the desire every single time. Just like he'd squelched his desire to stay in Merritt's Crossing.

Macey and Charlotte needed him to put aside his juvenile hobbies and focus on the future. Their future. He shifted his attention back to his phone and started his message to Landon.

The hum of a vehicle approaching outside interrupted him. Jack sighed and looked out the window again. His sister, Skye, and her husband, Gage, eased their blue SUV to a stop in front of his house. Skye had offered to bring lunch over so Connor could meet his new cousins. Except he'd forgotten to mention this to Laramie. Oh, well. She and Skye talked all the time. They'd probably traded plenty of texts already.

He quickly finished the message to Landon.

Hey, man. Congrats on another win. That last ride was epic. Sorry to hear about your grandfather. Let me know how I can help. FYI, Skye is throwing me a birthday party. July 3 at 3pm. Stop by if you're in town.

Jack hesitated, his finger hovering over the send icon. What would Laramie say if she knew he was texting her brother? He was probably crossing a line here, and she'd have a few choice words for him when she found out. If she found out. She was too stubborn to ask Landon for help, though. Jack had to do something. Ignoring the doubts battling inside, he sent the message, then pocketed his phone as Connor ran across the gravel and bounded up Jack's stairs. Laramie might be aggravated at first, but she'd thank him once Landon offered to help.

Chapter Six

"I still can't believe my brother has twins and my best friend is his nanny." Skye flashed a mischievous smile and reached for her strawberry-banana smoothie. "What else did I miss while I was on vacation?"

I'm officially falling in love with your brother. And his babies, too. Laramie tried for a casual shrug, then sucked another generous sip of her frozen mocha through her straw. The first part was hardly news. Laramie had told Skye about her feelings for Jack a long time ago. But her affection for Charlotte and Macey grew by leaps and bounds the longer she cared for them. How in the world would she ever be able to say goodbye to Jack *and* the babies?

"Did you know he wants to move to Utah?"

Skye's expression grew serious. "I heard."

"He already applied for a job." Even saying the words out loud sent Laramie's thoughts careening into panic mode. She squirmed in her chair next to a window at Common Grounds, the only coffee shop in Merritt's Crossing and one of her favorite places to hang out. Today the cozy seating, upbeat music streaming through the overhead speakers and conversation with her best friend did little to soothe her tangled emotions.

"How do you feel about his plans?" Skye prodded gently.

"He's making a huge mistake."

"Agreed," Skye said. "I'm still adjusting to the fact that he's a father of two. It's hard to fathom why he wants to move away from everything he's ever known. Then again, Uncle Kenny and Dad's deaths hit Jack hard. I don't think any of us realized how much he has struggled with the loss."

Laramie took another sip of her drink and casually glanced at the group of women hanging out on the couches near the fireplace. They all went to church with the Tomlinsons and her family. The girl wiping down a table nearby and the barista working behind the counter were both her students. While Skye knew how Laramie felt about Jack, she didn't need all of Merritt's Crossing knowing she was in love with someone who couldn't wait to leave town.

"I wish he had talked to someone about his problems instead of running off to Vegas and getting some girl pregnant."

Skye's eyes widened.

Oh my. Had she said that out loud? So much for being discreet. And since when had she become so jealous and judgmental?

"I'm sorry." Laramie reached over and clasped Skye's arm. "That was completely uncalled for. Please forgive me. I don't know why I said that."

"Because it's the truth. You don't need to apologize. We're all thinking the same thing. Jack hasn't always had the best coping strategies. Remember what happened whenever his team lost a basketball game in high school?"

"Yeah, he'd hurl baseballs at my grandfather's barn until his arm was so sore he couldn't lift it the next day." Laramie shook her head. "So hardheaded."

Skye arched an eyebrow, then drained the last of her smoothie.

"I'm nowhere near as stubborn as Jack," Laramie protested.

"It's a toss-up."

Before she could argue, her phone chimed. She picked it up and glanced at the screen. A message from Jack. He'd sent a video of Charlotte crawling across his living room.

Laramie gasped, then showed Skye. "Charlotte is crawling."

Skye offered a knowing smile. "That's great."

"What?" Laramie played the video again, then reluctantly put her phone down. She could watch that all day. Instead, she shifted her focus to Skye. "What are you not saying?"

Skye shrugged. "It's interesting that Jack sent you the video of Charlotte's milestone moment, that's all."

"He was excited to tell someone." Her fingers itched to send Jack a message. She reached for her drink instead, just to prove to Skye—and herself—that the video wasn't a big deal.

"And that someone is you." Skye grinned triumphantly. "You're allowed to have feelings about Jack, you know. Please don't worry about what people will say or think, either."

Laramie sighed. "If I'm honest, my feelings for Jack

have only grown stronger since I've started taking care of the girls."

Skye clapped her hands softly, eyes gleaming.

"Wait. Don't get too excited. The fact that he suddenly has two babies is hard for me to get used to. As much as I like taking care of the girls, I don't want to move to Utah. Ever. Remember what happened when I followed Zeke to Montana? That was a disaster. I promised myself I'd never move for a guy again."

"This is different, though."

"Different how?" Laramie jammed her straw deeper into the ice inside her drink. "I'd have to start over in a new place, make new friends, find a new job. Not to mention leaving my family and my volleyball team without a coach right before the season starts. Why should I uproot and follow him if he isn't interested in a relationship? What about what I need? I'm tired of putting everyone else's needs before my own. And besides, he didn't ask me."

"I totally get why you're scared, but I also love my brother very much, and you're my dearest friend. I want you both to be happy. Together." Skye's expression morphed from empathetic to all-business as she leaned closer. "You'd better tell each other how you feel before it's too late."

"I'm not making the first move." Except for falling apart in his arms yesterday. That wasn't exactly a move. More like poor judgment. She didn't have the energy to go there with Skye right now. Laramie linked her arms over her chest. "Call me stubborn, hardheaded, old-fashioned, whatever. I want to be pursued, and if he cared about me as anything more than his friend, wouldn't he have taken me on a date instead of asking me to be his nanny?"

"Maybe he thinks he isn't good enough for you."

"Well, maybe he's right. Maybe he isn't." Laramie shouldered her purse as she slid out of her chair. "I've got to go. I need to stop by the church and make the final arrangements for our car wash fundraiser this Saturday."

"Good to see you." Skye waved. "We'll talk soon."

Laramie made her way to the door, eager to get to the church and double-check the details for the volleyball team's fundraiser before the administrative assistant went to lunch. Abandoning Skye's words wasn't quite so easy, though. Did Skye and her family really want to see Jack and Laramie in a relationship?

Not that it mattered what his family wanted. Jack never did let that influence his choices. He seemed to go the opposite direction. And dwelling on her feelings for him wouldn't change anything. He planned to leave as soon as he could, while she couldn't possibly abandon her family now.

A baby who'd learned to crawl was highly overrated. Jack huffed out a breath as he gently guided Charlotte out from under his coffee table for what seemed like the bazillionth time. Yesterday, he'd sent Laramie the video of Charlotte on her hands and knees, awkwardly crawling across the living room floor while Jack cheered her on. Today the little stinker had gained confidence quickly. Too quickly. While part of him was happy she'd achieved a milestone, most of him was already exhausted keeping up with her. All hope of getting any work done this morning had vanished.

"You're quite pleased with yourself, aren't you?" Jack kissed her cheek, then set her back in the middle of the room.

"Ba-ba-ba-ba!" She grinned up at him, then pushed onto all fours and crawled right back toward the table.

Sweet mercy. Nap time couldn't get here soon enough. Refusing to be ignored, Macey bounced up and down nearby in the saucer thing with all the toys rimming the edge. She alternated between chewing on a plastic teddy bear's ear and screeching as loud as she could.

Jack massaged his temple and checked the time on his phone. Where was Laramie, anyway? She'd gone to buy more sponges and buckets for her car wash fundraiser and said she'd be back around lunch. It was almost twelve thirty. Maybe she ran into a friend at the hardware store. He could feed the girls on his own, but that didn't mean he wanted to. He'd have to get used to doing things on his own, though. Especially if he moved away.

An ache settled in his gut. Could he handle starting over in Utah with two babies? He squelched the doubt as soon as it arrived and crossed the room to help Macey. Staying in Merritt's Crossing wasn't the answer, either. Not when he collided with people's impossible expectations of him at every turn.

"What's the matter, sweet girl?" Maybe she was hungry. Or annoyed that he'd plopped her in the stationary toy. She hadn't quite figured out how to crawl, and she seemed aggravated that Charlotte was on the move. Did sibling competition start this early? He'd have to ask Laramie. She was the expert on all that child development stuff.

Charlotte grabbed a pink-and-purple rattle and thrust it into the air. The beads inside swirled around, capturing Macey's attention. She shrieked, then stretched out both arms, her little face crumpling in frustration.

Jack glanced at Charlotte, who shook the rattle again, almost as if she was taunting her sister, then shoved one end in her mouth. Macey burst into tears.

"Charlotte." He frowned at her. "Did you do that on purpose?"

She stared up at him, wide-eyed, still gnawing on the rattle.

While she wasn't formulating words yet, she'd certainly figured out how to annoy her sister with her actions.

Macey sobbed and bounced up and down in the saucer. Pitiful tears slid down her rosy cheeks.

"Aww, come here." He carefully lifted her up and snuggled her close.

Facing the window, he gently patted Macey's back and stared at the combine rolling across his neighbor's field. The fruity scent of her baby shampoo enveloped him as she sucked her thumb and nestled her head against his shoulder. A wisp of her hair tickled his chin.

Oh, brother. The hair. Thankfully he had a couple of years until he had to deal with bows, clips and braids. What was he going to do when they wanted braids? The thought of trying to figure out how to twist hair into a decent style was enough to make him break out in a cold sweat. And he couldn't even think about sleepovers, boyfriends or teaching them both to drive.

Macey heaved a sigh, then went limp in his arms. He glanced down as her eyelids fluttered closed. So much for feeding her lunch before her nap. Jack turned around and found Charlotte sitting beside the coffee table, ripping pages out of his latest outdoor adventure magazine.

Oh, well. At least she was sitting still. He didn't have time to read the thing, anyway.

It was amazing how two tiny humans had ransacked his life in the best possible way. He wasn't sleeping much, and he'd spent a small fortune on diapers and formula, but he'd also learned what it meant to love in a way he'd never understood or known before. Sure, the babies were exasperating, and he had no idea what he was doing half the time. Okay, more like eighty-five percent of the time. But he loved them no matter what.

Macey and Charlotte were *his*.

While he'd made a huge mistake when he chose to spend the weekend in Vegas with their mother, maybe the babies arriving on his doorstep meant God was giving him an opportunity to redeem his reckless, impulsive choices. A fierce determination to protect his daughters crested inside. He'd do everything possible to make sure his babies had what they needed to grow and thrive.

The morning sun showed no mercy as Laramie gathered her volleyball team in the church parking lot for a car wash. She was taking the whole team to camp at the university in Fort Collins next month, and this was their last fundraiser. Sweat slicked her skin and the heat radiating off the asphalt made her feel like she'd stepped inside an oven. Note to self—plan ahead next time and sell Christmas wreaths when the weather was cooler.

At least the girls had positive attitudes. Hers could use a serious adjustment, preferably in the form of a large iced coffee from Common Grounds. Ever since

Jack broke the news that his first interview had gone well and he was scheduled for a second, she hadn't been sleeping much.

Would it be wrong to leave Hope, the team's starting setter, in charge while she walked down the street to the coffee shop? Guilt pricked at her. One of the freshmen shrieked and hid behind her teammate as a senior playfully aimed a water hose at her. Yeah, probably better if she didn't leave them unsupervised.

"Girls. Focus, please." She gestured toward a minivan pulling into the parking lot. "Your first customer is here."

Two more cars trailed the minivan. Then a familiar pickup truck circled through the parking lot and joined the end of the line. She refused to look directly at the driver. There were other trucks like Jack's in town. Her palms instantly grew clammy and her insides did backflips like a cheerleader at a Friday night football game.

Laramie pretended to look after the girls while they splashed soapy sponges across the side of the minivan. Unfortunately for her, they didn't need a lot of instruction. She longed to steal a glance at Jack's truck. What was he doing here? She checked the time on her phone. The twins usually slept until ten thirty or so. Did he wake them from their naps to come to her team's car wash?

A few minutes later, the girls finished with the minivan and Hope collected the donation from the driver. Laramie smiled and waved at the man behind the wheel.

"Thank you for supporting our volleyball team," she said.

"Sure thing." He tipped his ball cap her direction, then drove away.

The next car—a teacher from the elementary school—pulled up. Laramie was so glad when she rolled down the window to chat for a minute. She needed a distraction.

"Good morning." Emily waggled her fingers. "How's it going?"

"Not bad." *Trying not to stare at the handsome single dad in the back of the line.* Laramie kept that thought to herself. "Thanks for coming by."

"Are you kidding?" Emily grinned. "I'm always glad to have my former students wash the dust off my car."

"I hear you." Laramie stepped back so the girls could get started, but Emily wasn't so easily deterred. "What's this I hear about you working as a nanny now? Are you still coaching volleyball or is this a permanent change?"

A dozen pair of eyes slid her way. Laramie was paralyzed. Was it temporary? She'd only planned to nanny for Jack for a few weeks. Until he'd pulled her into his arms. Again. She was still thinking about the warmth of his touch and the strength he'd—

"Coach?" Hope stared at her, holding the hose suspended over a bucket. The panic flashing in her eyes yanked Laramie back to reality.

"Completely temporary." Laramie held up her palm to confirm the validity of her words. "I'm helping Jack for a few weeks. It's an emergency. He'll find someone permanent when he…as soon as he can."

Oh boy. She was babbling. And she'd almost announced Jack's plans to move. Not that he wasn't moving—he'd made his intentions crystal clear. But it wasn't her place to announce his news here, especially to one of the chattiest women in all of Merritt's Crossing.

"He has twins, right?" Emily smirked. "I'd like to say I'm surprised, but he's always been quite the ladies' man."

Anger flared. She did not care for Emily's tone or her thinly veiled insult aimed at Jack.

"He's handling fatherhood quite well, actually." She forced her mouth into a polite smile. With all the girls still watching and listening to their conversation, she couldn't afford to say what was really on her mind. Firing back with a snide comment would do more harm than good.

"Hope, why don't you and the girls get started?" Laramie gestured to the line forming behind Emily. "We don't want to keep all these nice people waiting too long."

Emily waved and took another sip of her coffee, then rolled up her window. Laramie turned away, her skin heated. She'd jumped to Jack's defense rather quickly. Too quickly. Was Emily going to repeat their conversation to all her friends? And why did she even care?

Flustered, Laramie grabbed the vacuum and took out her frustrations on the next customer's interior. A few minutes later, she straightened and turned off the vacuum as Jack's truck eased in behind her.

Sweat trickled down her spine, making her T-shirt stick to her skin. She swiped the back of her hand across her forehead and met his gaze through the windshield. He waved, then motioned for her to come closer.

Laramie's heart hammered as she skirted the front of his truck and met him on the driver's side. Jack lowered his window.

"Hey." He handed her a large iced coffee. "I brought

this for you. The ladies at Common Grounds said this was your usual."

The familiar scent of his spicy aftershave greeted her, and his slow grin only made her heart rate skitter further out of control. *What in the world? It's just Jack in his stupid truck.*

"Thanks." Her voice was barely more than a squeak as she took the coffee.

"How's the car wash going?"

She lifted one shoulder, then popped the straw into the iced drink. Maybe caffeine would clear the fog from her muddled brain. "Good so far."

Minus the part where Emily grilled me and I defended you.

Jack's gaze flitted from her head to her toes and back. "I like your shirt. You look good in green."

The frozen mocha cooled her parched mouth and she almost choked as his words registered. Was he *flirting* with her?

Laramie coughed and Jack's brow furrowed.

"Is something wrong with your drink?"

"No, not at all. It's, um, good. Thank you." She cleared her throat, then peeked over his shoulder at the car seats behind him. "Are the girls with you?"

"Yeah. Why?"

"Did you wake them up early from their naps just to bring me coffee?"

Hurt flashed in Jack's eyes. "It's almost ninety-five degrees. I thought you'd appreciate a cold drink."

"I do. I said thank-you, right?" She blew out a breath. "Can we at least wash your truck? I feel bad that they're missing their naps."

Jack's smile was tight this time. "Nope, we only

came by to see you and bring coffee. I'll make a donation, though. Have a great day, Laramie."

He passed her a twenty-dollar bill then rolled up his window and slowly eased his car toward the exit.

As she watched him drive away, Hope elbowed her in the ribs. "Real smooth, Coach. Real smooth."

The other girls standing nearby didn't bother to stifle their laughter. Laramie cringed inwardly. She hadn't meant to be rude or sound ungrateful. He'd blindsided her with the coffee delivery and the not-so-subtle compliment. So not fair.

She kept staring long after his truck disappeared. *What are you up to, Jack?* If he was determined to move to Utah, why did he have to show up looking so good and flirting like he was interested in anything more than friendship?

Chapter Seven

Late Monday morning, Jack sat at his desk in his home office, staring at the email update from the recruiter for the job in Utah. The details regarding his second interview scheduled for next week filled the screen. Exactly what he'd hoped for. The position offered great benefits, there would be no traveling and the location was very family-friendly. So why was he hesitating?

An incoming call saved him from responding. He glanced at his phone sitting on the desk. His brother-in-law's name and number lit up the screen.

"Hello?"

"Hey. Have you got a minute?" Gage's voice was tight. "I need a favor."

"What's up?" Jack spun around in his chair, relieved he didn't have to think about why he wasn't more interested in the interview.

"Skye scheduled a delivery for today and I forgot all about it. I have an appointment I can't reschedule."

Jack groaned. "I see where this is going."

"She'll never leave me in charge of the store again if I mess this up."

"And that's a bad thing?" Jack couldn't resist giving his brother-in-law a hard time. Gage was a good sport about helping at the family's furniture store, but they all knew he was much better off as a wind energy technician.

Gage ignored his teasing and got right down to business. "I'm not above bribery. I just roped your brother into helping me out. Can you meet him at the customer's house to unload in fifteen minutes?"

"Do you have the truck?"

"Drew is backing it up to the loading dock now."

Jack glanced over his shoulder at the clock on his computer. Wasn't he looking for an excuse to avoid confirming the interview? He needed to eat lunch and Laramie had taken the twins to story time at the library, so he couldn't use his kids as a reason to say no, either.

"Single mom, local address. She'd really like to get settled in the house today so she doesn't have to spend another night in a hotel. I'll even throw in dinner at your favorite steakhouse to sweeten the deal."

Jack let out a low whistle at the mention of the nearest steakhouse. "Man, you are desperate."

"You have no idea."

"Text me the address and tell Drew I'll meet him there."

"Thanks, man," Gage said. "And thanks for keeping me out of trouble with Skye."

"No problem. I look forward to that steak dinner." He ended the call and strode down the hall toward the kitchen. Jack smiled as he stopped and surveyed the clean counters, high chairs wiped down and neatly tucked away, and the dishwasher humming softly. The scent of laundry detergent lingering in the air indicated another load was in the machine nearby. While he'd spent the twins' morning nap time in his office, Laramie had cleaned up the kitchen, kept the laundry going and basically restored order in his home. Not to mention prepared the girls for an outing and loaded them in their car seats without any help from him.

His smile faded. Was she keeping busy to avoid him? The niggling thought morphed into worry and he rubbed his palm against the tightness in his chest. Laramie was incredible. And so selfless, stepping in and helping him in his darkest hour. But she'd seemed distant and maybe even uncomfortable since he'd brought her coffee at the car wash. After all she'd done for him lately, stopping by with her favorite drink was the least he could do.

Except she'd acted less than thrilled when she saw him. Had he embarrassed her?

His phone chimed again and he quickly read the text from Drew with the address of the furniture delivery. Jack grabbed his keys and left the house.

Laramie had arrived right on time this morning, but the tension threading through the room while she fed the girls their oatmeal and pureed fruit bugged him. He was hyperaware of how good Laramie smelled, the little crease that formed in her brow when she was concentrating and the musical sound of her laughter when the twins blew her slobbery kisses. She was beautiful, she cared for his girls almost effortlessly, and his world was a thousand times better because she was in it.

So why had she looked at him like he had something growing in the middle of his forehead when he brought her coffee?

As Jack drove the short distance to meet Drew, he

carefully replayed their previous conversations, including everything he'd said at the car wash. Talking to a woman and flirting had never been a challenge before.

This was different. *He* was different. At least he wanted to be, anyway. While shallow relationships with low expectations was how he'd rolled through his twenties, those days were over. He turned thirty in less than a week, and he was a father of two. The best person he knew spent hours every day caring for his children, and making his house feel like a home, and he couldn't stop thinking about her as more than a friend.

Maybe that was the problem. He wanted what he could never have. Convincing Laramie to see him as anything more than her best friend's misguided, irresponsible brother was next to impossible. While he wanted to be the kind of man Laramie deserved, his track record screamed that he was the exact opposite.

No wonder she'd looked disgusted when he'd tried to flirt. His past couldn't be wiped away like baby food splattered across the high chair tray. Since Laramie had known him forever, his exploits were hardly a secret. And there wasn't a grand gesture, a compliment or anything that could change that reality.

Face it. You'll never be enough for her.

Jack sighed and parked his truck at the curb. He shut off the engine, tucked his phone in his pocket and stepped out into the blazing summer sun.

"Hey." Drew stood beside the delivery truck parked in front of a townhouse, two bottles of water in his hands. "Thanks for coming."

"Not a problem." Jack accepted one of the water bottles Drew offered and took a sip.

The truck's back door rumbled as Drew pushed it

open. Jack glanced at the furniture wrapped in blankets and cartons. There wasn't a lot. Hopefully this wouldn't take long. He had a phone call scheduled with a project manager at two o'clock.

Drew climbed inside the truck and unwrapped the first piece. "You know, you could build something like this."

Oh, here we go. Another Jack-needs-to-build-furniture pep talk. Jack eyed the coffee table with clean lines and two simple drawers, then forced a tight smile. "Thanks for the vote of confidence. Not interested. Furniture isn't my thing."

Drew's eyebrows shot up. "You loved hanging out with Dad and Uncle Kenny in their shop. Don't you remember helping them build McKenna's bedroom set?"

Jack gritted his teeth, determined to battle back the memory. Yeah, he remembered. And he'd had almost the same conversation with Dad, too. He wasn't interested in revisiting the heated words they'd exchanged.

"I have a job, and two girls to provide for now. I'll leave the furniture business to Skye."

Drew gave him a long stare. "That's a shame, letting all that talent go to waste."

Resentment flared in his stomach. Jack tightened his fists but let the comment slide. Although he wanted to pop off about how he was sick and tired of the unsolicited advice, he knew it wasn't worth it. People had their opinions and there was no sense trying to change their minds. As soon as they were finished with this delivery, Jack was going to accept that interview in Utah.

She could do this. Taking twins to summer story time at the library had seemed like such a good idea when Skye suggested it. Too bad Charlotte wasn't on board.

"Charlotte, listen," Laramie whispered, trying to re-direct Charlotte's attention toward the front of the room. While the librarian read a book about a duck riding a bike and the other parents sat on the blue carpet in a semicircle at her feet, their children quietly enthralled with the pictures and words, Charlotte had crawled to the nearest shelf and yanked board books off like it was her job. And Macey was already gnawing on her fist. Was she hungry again?

"Charlotte, stop." Laramie scrambled to put the books back while keeping an eye on both girls at once.

Two women sitting nearby whispered to one another, then shot disapproving looks Laramie's way. Great. Nothing like making a scene in front of the other parents. One of them was probably texting Jack right now, telling him he'd hired a lousy nanny.

Meanwhile, Charlotte crawled out of reach, while Macey started to cry. Laramie heaved a sigh. "Charlotte, no."

Charlotte squealed and picked up speed. Laramie scooped her up and confiscated the board book before Charlotte managed to put the corner in her mouth. The frustrated baby arched her back and released an ear-splitting screech.

Laramie tucked her into the double stroller and handed her a pacifier. "Shhh, it's okay."

Charlotte's crying escalated, drawing even more curious stares. Warmth heated her face as Laramie picked Macey up, snagged her diaper bag from the chair where she'd left it and quickly pushed the stroller toward the front door. Sweat beaded on her forehead as the twins' cries echoed through the library. She should be able to handle two babies having a meltdown in public, right?

Laramie burst through the automatic double doors of the library and out into the sweltering June afternoon. Charlotte and Macey were both crying now.

She pressed her palm to their foreheads. Not warm enough for a fever, but maybe they were teething? The tears clinging to their lashes and the pitiful crying made Laramie's heart ache. And she'd left their new teething rings in Jack's refrigerator. She dug through the diaper bag in search of toys that might soothe them on the car ride home.

"Everything okay?"

Gage Westbrook's voice startled her. Laramie glanced up. He hovered over the stroller, his sunglasses pushed on top of his head and brows knitted together.

"Hey, Gage." Laramie handed each of the babies a plastic toy. "I think they're both teething."

Gage sat beside her on the bench. "I was coming out of the doctor's office and heard the crying." He leaned closer and gave Macey's arm a gentle pat. "Sorry about your teeth, kiddo."

Macey's breath hitched and she stopped crying, her eyes riveted on Gage.

"Girls, can you say hello to your uncle Gage?"

"I like the sound of that." Gage grinned. "Although I still can't believe it's true."

"Me, either." An awkward silence lingered between them. Laramie didn't want to talk about Jack or his daughters or his plans right now. It hurt too much to think about a life in Merritt's Crossing that didn't include Jack and the twins. She cleared her throat and studied him. "What are you up to today?"

"I had my physical and now I'm going to stop by the bakery and order the cake for Jack's birthday party this weekend. You're coming, right?"

Laramie looked away. Skye had texted her the details for the thirtieth birthday party she and Gage were hosting. Laramie hadn't responded yet. Sweat trickled down her back. This heat was ridiculous. She needed to get the girls home for lunch and their afternoon nap.

"Laramie?"

"We'll see."

Gage's hazel eyes narrowed. "Everything okay?"

"Yeah, I'm just hot. Worried about the girls and their teething." *And Jack. And how weird things are between us now.* She'd keep that part to herself. Gage was a great guy and all, but there was no way she'd vent to him.

"I hear you," Gage said. "Connor cries a lot when he doesn't feel well. Jack's fortunate to have you helping him. He must be so glad to have you around."

Then why was he planning to leave? She bit back the pointed question. Giving voice to her feelings only led to more questions she couldn't answer.

"Has Jack mentioned anything to you about using some of those tools out in his woodshop? Skye says he's so good at building stuff, and he inherited a lot of tools."

"Jack hasn't said a word about building anything. He never goes into the shop, either."

"Really."

"Have you and Skye asked him to build anything?" Laramie checked on the girls. They were happily gnawing on their toys and watching the people and cars moving in and out of the library parking lot.

"Not lately." Gage frowned. "She says the last time she brought it up, he got upset."

Laramie nodded. "He was really close to his dad and his uncle. I'm not sure he's ever fully grieved their deaths."

Gage stared at the ground. "I know what that's like."

Laramie remained silent. Gage had lost his best friend in a terrible fire when they were in the navy together. While that accident brought him to Merritt's Crossing, eventually marrying Skye and becoming Connor's father, she knew he'd worked through a lot of grief and guilt, too.

"Maybe Jack and I can grab a burger sometime and talk more." Gage stood. "I'd better get going."

"Me, too." Laramie stood and reached for the girls' stroller.

"So we'll see you at Jack's party then?" Gage asked. She hesitated.

"Cake. Homemade ice cream. Chocolate syrup. Whipped cream and sprinkles. What more can I say to convince you?"

Laughter bubbled up. "All right, all right. I'll be there. Thank you for the reminder."

"You're welcome." Gage waved to his nieces, then walked down the street toward his truck.

Laramie pushed the stroller along the sidewalk to her own car, then buckled the girls in their car seats and stowed the bulky stroller in the trunk. Sweaty and exhausted, she slid behind the wheel and cranked the air-conditioning as high as it could go. Had she just said yes to Jack's birthday party? She didn't want to stay home, but at the same time, going made her feel as nervous as a middle schooler at her first dance. Right on cue, butterflies flitted through her abdomen. She wasn't ready to admit that her feelings for Jack were changing. And that she secretly entertained notions of a happily-ever-after and a future Jack was not interested in being a part of. He was going to move and take Macey and Charlotte with him. All she'd have to cling to were some sweet memories and the old familiar heartache of being single and childless at thirty-four.

"What's in the building out back?"

Jack froze, a spoonful of pureed peaches halfway to Charlotte's mouth. The question seemed innocent, but he knew Laramie well enough to know there was a reason she was asking. "Stuff that belonged to my aunt and uncle. Why?"

"I saw Gage outside the library today and he mentioned you had a bunch of tools to build furniture stored in there that you never use."

He sensed her staring at him from her seat beside Macey's high chair, where she was serving an identical bowl of pureed fruit. Her gaze was warm. Curious. But he still didn't want to talk about the woodshop or the tools inside or analyze all the reasons why he never went in there. Couldn't they focus on feeding the girls, giving them baths and the countless other tasks required to put two babies in bed? Macey and Charlotte had fussed constantly since they woke up from their afternoon naps. He was counting the minutes until they both went to bed for the night.

"McKenna and Aunt Willa included the shop and everything inside when they sold me the house. I've never planned on building anything, though. Just never got around to sorting it all out."

Because he never wanted to.

He scraped the plastic spoon along the bottom of the container and offered Charlotte another bite.

"I remember the bedroom set you built for McKenna." Laramie cleaned Macey's fingers with a damp cloth. "She was so happy."

What in the world? Why was everyone in his life suddenly rooting for him to build something?

"I helped," he said, fighting to keep irritation from his voice. "Dad and my uncle did most of the work."

"That's not how I remember it, but you get credit for being humble."

If they were talking about any other topic, he would've appreciated Laramie's attempt at humor. This time his limbs tingled with the urge to run.

"Ba-ba-ba." Charlotte grinned then blew raspberries, sprinkling his cheek with pureed fruit.

"Hey." Jack swiped the back of his hand across his face. "That wasn't cool."

Laramie clapped a hand over her mouth and her shoulders shook as she tried to smother her laughter.

Undeterred, Charlotte grinned and blew more raspberries.

Irritation flared in his gut. He had to get out of here.

"I need a minute." Jack shoved his chair back, stomped across the kitchen and out the sliding glass door. The summer evening air blanketed him, carrying a hint of earth and dust from the wheat harvest in the fields nearby. He paced the deck, his legs eating up the wooden planks. In the distance, wind turbines spun against a dusky blue sky. Blood pounded behind his ears. He'd almost lost his temper. Reacted to a baby's harmless antics in a way he'd deeply regret later. Why did he let Charlotte's behavior get to him?

Jack turned away from that stupid building taunting him and sank into an Adirondack chair. He leaned forward, bracing his head in his hands.

A few minutes later, the slider glided open and the deck vibrated with Laramie's footsteps.

"I put the babies in the portable crib in the living room for a few minutes." She pulled another chair up next to his. "Are you all right?"

Her presence calmed him. Like he was surfacing from a deep dive into the lake. Being with Laramie was like a giant gulp of clean, fresh mountain air.

"I can't do this."

She sat down. "Do what?"

He longed to grab her hand and thread his fingers through hers. Oh, he needed an anchor right now. Someone to cling to. "Keep living here in this fishbowl of a town, with everyone and their brother weighing in on how I live my life."

"We all have bad days. Babies are exhausting, and you have twins. Don't let people get to you."

Jack scrubbed his palm across his face and stared out into the fields.

"What happened today that made you so upset?"

"I've heard one too many comments lately from my family about building furniture. I know they don't really want my help, though, because they've always blamed me for my dad's accident."

Laramie's gasp was audible. "That is so not true."

Jack glanced at her in the gathering twilight. The setting sun cast an orange-and-pink glow across the planes of her face. Man, she was gorgeous. He forced himself to look away. If he was too distracted, he wouldn't be able to say what was on his mind. And these emotions

were eating him alive. He had to tell someone. Someone who would genuinely listen.

"My dad was angry about my decision to go into
cybersecurity. He wanted me to take over the parts of
the business Uncle Kenny used to handle. I said no. We
yelled. He threw a chair across the shop. That was the
last time we spoke to each other. He died a few hours
later."

"I'm so sorry. I know how much your father and your
uncle meant to you." Laramie leaned over and gently
squeezed his forearm. "Please, please hear me when
I say that no one blames you for your father's death."

He welcomed the warmth of her touch on his skin,
and his fingers itched to blanket hers with his own.
Jack wanted to believe her. Laramie's friendship with
Skye meant she'd witnessed the ripple effects of his
uncle's suicide and his father's death. But he'd seen the
hurt and regret and disappointment in his own mother's
eyes. Pete and the rest of his dad's friends reminded
him every time he passed their booth at the diner that
he wasn't living up to his potential.

"Here's the thing. My dad was a master manipulator,
drove his brother to commit suicide and almost left my
mother in financial ruin. So why would I want any part
of a business that wreaked havoc on our family? My
relationships with my siblings and Gage mean more to
me than building a table or a dresser."

"What if you could have both? The opportunity to
work with your hands and have healthy relationships.
It's possible, you know."

"I don't want both," he grumbled. "Everything's fine
the way it is."

"Is it?"

Those two little words needled him. If everything was fine, why was he melting down on his deck?

"Are you happy, Jack?"

I'm happy when I'm with you.

What if he had the courage to say those words out loud right now? Laramie made him laugh, challenged his thinking, took great care of his daughters. She didn't judge him or run when he was coming unglued. But he couldn't tell her how his feelings for her had changed, because once he crossed that line from friendship to something more, there was no going back.

The babies' crying saved him from answering. For once, he was grateful for their timing.

"I'll get them," Laramie said.

"You don't have to." Jack stood but she blocked his path. "You've been with them all day."

She turned and strode toward the door. "I'll leave as soon as they're in bed."

Jack sat back down. Selfishly, he'd take all the help she offered. Especially tonight. He glanced over his shoulder and watched as she slipped through the sliding screen door, then lifted Macey out of the portable crib.

Macey fit nicely on Laramie's hip and stopped crying immediately.

Jack sighed. What was he going to do without Laramie? He couldn't stay in Merritt's Crossing, but how could he ask her to leave her home, her family and her job for him?

Laramie hated seeing Jack like this. Wrecked. Defeated.

I know they don't really want my help...

A sickening feeling settled in her stomach. Jack thought his family didn't want him around. Laramie snuck a glance at Jack feeding Macey on the opposite end of the sofa. His mouth turned down in a frown as he held her bottle with the baby snuggled in the crook of his arm.

Did he honestly believe that he was responsible for his father's death? What a horrible burden. She'd never heard Skye or Drew or Mrs. Tomlinson say anything like that, but they had made plenty of comments about Jack shirking responsibility. Even though they might've laced their comments with humor, Jack was clearly hurt. And maybe that was why he didn't show up at many family gatherings anymore. Laramie had listened to Skye vent her frustrations when she'd moved home to help their mom during her recovery from surgery and Jack hardly helped at all.

Like a moth to a flame, Laramie glanced at Jack again. Macey's hair was still damp from her bath and her eyelids were heavy as she slurped down the last of the formula. If Jack noticed Laramie was staring, he didn't meet her gaze, so she let her eyes travel to the corded muscles in Jack's forearm as he tenderly supported Macey. His black T-shirt was a sharp contrast to the baby's white pajamas with pink polka dots. Laramie captured a mental snapshot of Jack caring for his daughter.

She sighed and dragged her gaze away. If she wasn't careful, she'd melt into a pathetic puddle and say all kinds of things she'd only regret later. Despite his self-doubts and the grief and guilt he was obviously wrestling with, moments like these gave her glimpses of a different side of Jack. He was capable of being an attentive father. So maybe he had a long track record of being irresponsible and not showing up for his family, but at least he was trying with his girls. Should she speak up? Tell him that she was proud of him for accepting his role as a single parent of twins?

She glanced at Charlotte snuggled in her arms, taking her dear sweet time finishing her bottle, but thankfully her eyes were slowly closing. Charlotte had fussed and resisted her bath and exhausted all of Laramie's patience as she helped get the babies ready for bed. Her phone buzzed next to her on the arm of the sofa and Charlotte's eyes sprang open.

No, no, no. Laramie willed her to not start fussing again. That text was probably from Skye, asking why Laramie was late for their girls' night out. She craned her neck to check the time on her phone's screen. Only fifteen minutes late. Not a big deal. If she was honest, she wanted the babies to go to sleep and she secretly hoped Jack asked her to stay a little longer. Her imagination took that idea and ran with it. Maybe they'd watch a movie. Or just hang out and talk. Sure, taking care of two infants all day had depleted her physically. But sitting here with Jack, feeding the babies, cocooned in the warmth of his house and the innocent fragrance of lavender baby shampoo lingering in the air, it was hard to leave.

Stop. Why bail on a night out with friends because Jack had a bad day? That was exactly the kind of enabling behavior she'd vowed to avoid. Wasn't it? Besides, Jack was giving zero indication that he had any intention of asking her to stick around. He'd already encouraged her to leave once the girls' baths were finished.

Her phone chimed again with another text. Laramie banished all thoughts of spending the rest of the evening with Jack. As soon as the twins were in bed, she was leaving.

Finally, Charlotte finished her bottle. Laramie set it on the coffee table and Charlotte heaved a contented sigh, her long eyelashes fluttering against her cheek. Laramie stood, draped a cloth over her shoulder and gently helped the baby burp. She reached for her phone and tucked it in the back pocket of her jeans. Her leg brushed against Jack's knee as she scooted past him on the way to the girls' bedroom.

"I'm going to put her down, then I have to go," she whispered.

He didn't even look up. His nod was almost imperceptible.

She glared at the top of his head. Like falling in the dunk tank at the county fair, irritation doused the feelings of contentment and attraction that had kindled a few minutes ago. Was a little gratitude too much to expect?

Laramie gently placed Charlotte in the portable crib, flicked on the white noise machine, then strode down the hall. She snagged her purse from the kitchen counter, double-checked her keys were inside, then slipped out the front door without saying goodbye.

And Jack didn't even notice.

Outside, the horizon burned red with the remnants of the sunset, and a million stars twinkled across the indigo sky. Summer nights were her favorite. Normally, Laramie would pause and inhale a deep breath of the warm evening air. Instead, gravel crunched under her boots today as she hurried to her car.

Sometimes Jack made her so mad she wanted to scream. He couldn't feed and bathe his babies without help, so why was he was still thinking about moving? Even following through with the interview process was ridiculous at this point. Okay, so maybe his family had said some hurtful things in the past. While their delivery wasn't great, their intentions were good. Everyone who cared about Jack, including her, was tired of watching him be miserable. Why did he still think leaving town was the solution to his problems? What about Macey and Charlotte? What about all those things the social worker had told him about introducing too much change in their lives and helping them bond?

He'd acted like he was taking the social worker's advice, but now he railed against it. She forced back an unwanted lump of emotion rising in her throat. Letting him persuade her to be his nanny had been a mistake. Although she'd never been able to turn away from a human in need, she needed to establish boundaries if for no other reason than to protect her heart.

Chapter Eight

"Happy Birthday!"

Jack stood in the middle of Skye and Gage's back deck, holding a car seat in each hand, and trying not to glare at the silver-haired man standing way too close to his mom. He was supposed to be smiling and thanking his family and clapping a few shoulders, but the only thought running through his head was *Mom brought a date to my birthday party?*

"Jack?" Skye moved closer, her smile wavering. "Say something."

He cleared his throat, but no words came.

Charlotte squealed and kicked, rocking the car seat. Jack tightened his grip on the handle and kept staring. The man said something to Laramie's parents, which made his mom lean even closer and squeeze the arm of his pastel-pink button-down. Who wore a pink button-down to an ice cream party in July, anyway? His mom's laughter rang out and Jack ground his teeth. Some stranger was making her laugh like she hadn't in a long time, and he didn't like it. Not one bit.

"Hey." Skye stood in front of him. Her uncertain

gaze scanned his face. "Are you all right? You said an afternoon party sounded great. We thought you'd love a big bash. I mean—" she gestured to the car seats "—probably not a bash like you'd prefer, but we wanted to celebrate your big day anyway."

Ah, yes, a big-sister jab at his former carefree days. "The party's great, sis. Thanks." He forced a smile, then tipped his chin toward their mom. "Who is the guy standing beside Mom?"

"Happy Birthday, Jack." Gage strode by with their son, Connor, riding on his shoulders.

"Hi, Grandma!" Connor yelled across the yard.

Laughter rippled through the group gathered on the lawn.

The man with Jack's mother smiled and greeted Gage with a friendly handshake. Jack's breath hitched. Connor leaned forward and gave his grandmother's new boyfriend an enthusiastic high five.

Jack shot Skye a pointed look. "You've met him already."

It was a statement instead of a question, and he didn't even bother to conceal his accusatory tone.

Skye avoided his gaze. Instead, she reached into the car seat, walked her fingers up Charlotte's tummy and tapped the baby's nose, eliciting a bubbly giggle. Skye laughed and repeated the process, earning more adorable squeals. Usually Jack couldn't resist that kind of happiness from his daughters. Except today. He couldn't get over the fact that his mother had brought *him* here.

"We had dinner last night," Skye said. "He's super nice."

Super nice. All righty, then. That made the whole scenario peachy keen, didn't it?

Jack battled back the snarky comments. His sister had thrown him a birthday party. Now was not the time to say what he was really thinking. But wasn't she the least bit concerned about who their mother was spending time with?

"Want me to hold the girls while you say hello?"

"Nope." Not interested. There would be plenty of time for his mother to make introductions. Besides, he'd brought twins to a party when neither baby had napped well. He was already in way over his head.

"There's a portable crib set up for you." Skye motioned to a corner of the yard under a huge tree. "Macey and Charlotte can take turns in the baby swing we borrowed from a friend. I'll ask Gage to bring it out on the deck."

Jack looked past Skye's shoulder in time to make eye contact with Laramie. Her smile was tight as she tucked a strand of hair behind her ear. His gaze traveled from her long platinum hair to her leather earrings shaped liked feathers, and the mint-green T-shirt she'd paired with white pants. His pulse sped. She looked amazing. As always. After the girls went down for their naps, she'd left his house to get ready for the party. Seeing Laramie here was already the best part of the whole afternoon. Surrounded by her family and friends, she glowed with contentment.

He was instantly jealous of his friend Cooper, who was talking to her, and wished he was the one standing beside her now.

"If you need a break, I can find someone to help. It's hard to take care of two babies and—"

"Skye." Jack silenced her with a gentle squeeze

on her arm. "Thank you. For everything. You're so thoughtful."

"We're more than happy to throw a party for you, Jack." Skye smiled. "Happy birthday."

He was thrown off-kilter by her words. Other than the comment about a bash, this was the most enjoyable interaction he'd had with his sister in a long time. "You don't have to stand here with me," he said. "I know you want to say hello to everyone."

Macey's babbling grew louder while Charlotte's screeching was drawing some curious stares from other guests.

Skye's brows arched.

"I've got this. Honest." He angled his head toward the people standing in her backyard. "Go have fun."

"All right." She hesitated, still hovering. "I'll be around if you need me."

"I won't." He was such a liar. If she stood there another second, he was going to take her up on her offer and tuck a grumpy baby in her arms.

Jack sank to his knees and unbuckled Charlotte first. Man, he'd miscalculated. He'd learned how to care for both babies at the same time, but only when they were sleepy. What was he thinking, bringing them along? He should've hired a babysitter. As he pushed to his feet with Charlotte in his arms, both girls were crying. Panic flamed in his gut and he whirled around, hating himself for telling his sister he didn't need her help.

Emily, an elementary school teacher and a woman he'd dated a few times but never called again, strode toward him wearing a white sleeveless blouse, heels and a denim mini skirt. Her lipstick was too red and her perfume overbearing as she stretched out her arms. "Come say hello to me, little one."

"Here." Jack didn't even bother with a greeting. He just leaned close, letting her take Charlotte from him. Immediately, the baby stopped crying, no doubt captivated by the fistful of Emily's long hair she'd just grabbed.

He was kneeling to unbuckle Macey from her car seat when he caught a glimpse of a white cowboy hat through Gage and Skye's sliding door. Then voices rose, Emily gasped and the boards on the deck vibrated as Landon Chambers made his grand entrance.

"Jack, my man." Landon's too-white smile split his tanned face. Was he a bull rider or an influencer for a teeth-whitening product?

"Hey, Landon." Jack flinched as Landon smacked him on the shoulder. "Thanks for coming."

"Wouldn't miss it." Landon braced his hands on his waist. "Happy Birthday."

"Thanks."

Landon's boot-cut jeans looked like they'd come from an upscale shop in Denver. The short sleeves on his pearl-snap button-down were so snug his arms practically bulged against the fabric. If Jack wasn't so worried about what Laramie was thinking right now, he'd probably laugh at how much Landon had changed. Something niggled in his gut, warning him that she was not happy to see her brother.

While Emily held Charlotte and flirted shamelessly with Landon, a flash of white and mint green caught Jack's attention. Laramie cut long strides across the yard, then disappeared around the side of the house.

"I'll be right back." Jack left Macey in her car seat,

Charlotte in Emily's arms and pushed past Landon. He leaped off the deck's steps and jogged across the yard.

"Laramie, wait."

He didn't care who saw him or what they thought about him running after her. She was like a ray of sunshine and he couldn't imagine getting through the rest of the afternoon without her.

"Ouch." Laramie winced and glanced down at her new shoes. The silver sandals with the wedge heels had seemed like a good idea when she'd slipped them on, but now the straps cut into her skin and derailed her quick exit from the party.

Her stupid brother just had to show up like this party was meant for him and hog the spotlight. Who invited him, anyway? Her parents hadn't said a word about Landon coming home. According to social media, he was supposed to be at some big event in Texas. She gritted her teeth as she hurried across the street to the park in Skye and Gage's neighborhood.

One minute, Laramie was sipping lemonade and talking with Cooper, the next she was glaring daggers at Emily while she flirted with Jack and pretended to like babies. Charlotte wasn't a newborn and she hated to be held the way Emily had her—cradled like a football. Facing out so she could see what was going on kept her happiest. Laramie was about to intervene and rescue Jack and the twins from Emily when her brother had showed up. Somebody should tell him that white cowboy hat looked ridiculous.

"Laramie, please."

Jack's voice drifted toward her. She refused to turn around, although she did have to stop running. Her feet were killing her and she was surrounded by a playground, two picnic tables and a basketball court. She'd left her purse, car keys and phone in Skye and Gage's guest room because she'd planned on staying late to help clean up after the party. It was too far to walk home, especially in these sandals, and she wasn't about to ask Jack to give her a ride.

"Can we talk?"

She ignored him and sat down at the picnic table. He stopped a few feet away, his chest heaving as he caught his breath. Laramie leaned over, unbuckled the sandals then tossed them in the grass. Mercy. Sweet relief.

"Any particular reason why you left the party?"

"Any particular reason why you followed me?" She stood and moved toward the swing set, the grass cool against the soles of her feet. Okay, that was snarky and probably uncalled for, since Jack was the only person who cared that she'd left.

She sat on the swing and gripped the metal links in each hand. The black vinyl seat was probably going to ruin her white pants. She sat down anyway. Jack claimed the swing next to hers. His gaze warmed her skin. She still refused to look at him. Planting her toe in the dirt, she pushed off, the chains squeaking as she started to swing.

"Is this about Landon?"

"I can't believe he was invited."

Jack cleared his throat. "That's my fault."

She glared at him. "How?"

"I sent a message telling him I was sorry to hear about your grandfather and congratulated him on his last ride. I also mentioned today's party."

"You did what?" Blood pounded in her head. "Why?"

FREE BOOKS GIVEAWAY

2 FREE **ROMANCE** BOOKS!

2 FREE **SUSPENSE** BOOKS!

GET UP TO FOUR FREE BOOKS & TWO FREE GIFTS WORTH OVER $20!

We pay for everything!

Complete the survey below and return it today to receive up to 4 FREE BOOKS and FREE GIFTS guaranteed!

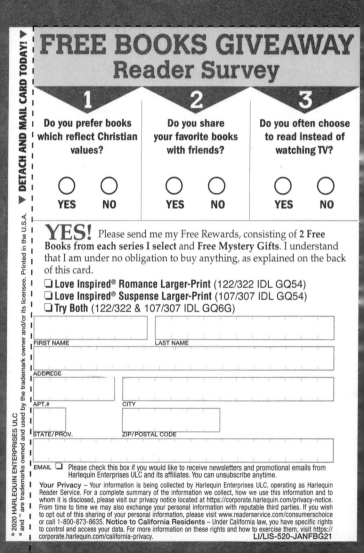

FREE BOOKS GIVEAWAY
Reader Survey

1
Do you prefer books which reflect Christian values?

◯ YES   ◯ NO

2
Do you share your favorite books with friends?

◯ YES   ◯ NO

3
Do you often choose to read instead of watching TV?

◯ YES   ◯ NO

YES! Please send me my Free Rewards, consisting of **2 Free Books from each series I select** and **Free Mystery Gifts**. I understand that I am under no obligation to buy anything, as explained on the back of this card.

❏ Love Inspired® Romance Larger-Print (122/322 IDL GQ54)
❏ Love Inspired® Suspense Larger-Print (107/307 IDL GQ54)
❏ Try Both (122/322 & 107/307 IDL GQ6G)

FIRST NAME	LAST NAME

ADDRESS

APT.#	CITY

STATE/PROV.	ZIP/POSTAL CODE

EMAIL ❏ Please check this box if you would like to receive newsletters and promotional emails from Harlequin Enterprises ULC and its affiliates. You can unsubscribe anytime.

LI/LIS-520-JANFBG21

HARLEQUIN READER SERVICE—Here's how it works:

BUSINESS REPLY MAIL
FIRST-CLASS MAIL   PERMIT NO. 717   BUFFALO, NY

POSTAGE WILL BE PAID BY ADDRESSEE

HARLEQUIN READER SERVICE
PO BOX 1341
BUFFALO NY 14240-8571

NO POSTAGE
NECESSARY
IF MAILED
IN THE
UNITED STATES

▲ If offer card is missing write to: Harlequin Reader Service, P.O. Box 1341, Buffalo, NY 14240-8531 or visit www.ReaderService.com ▲

"Because your family needs help with the wheat harvest and getting the right care for your grandfather."

"Nobody asked you to do that, Jack." Laramie couldn't keep the anger from her voice. She let the swing slow down, then jumped off, grimacing as the pebbles in the dirt nipped at her skin. Behind her, Jack abandoned his swing and caught up as she paced the lawn beside the picnic table.

"He didn't respond, so I assumed he wasn't coming," Jack said. "That's why I never mentioned anything to you."

"Landon ruins everything," she whispered.

"He does?" Jack frowned. "What do you mean?"

Laramie slumped on the picnic table bench. A warm breeze rippled the fabric of her T-shirt. She refused to look at him. *Go. Away.* She dug her nails into her palms and willed him to leave her alone. Then she wouldn't have to explain why she'd just spouted the most childish words ever.

"Nothing. It's—never mind." Inexplicable tears stung the backs of her eyelids and she ducked her head, trying to hide behind a curtain of hair. The bench shifted as Jack sank down beside her.

"I'm sorry, Laramie." He rested his palm on her forearm. "The last thing I ever want to do is upset you."

"Yeah, well, too late."

"Your feelings matter to me and you left my party. As the guest of honor, I'd like to know why."

Did she owe him an explanation? And where would she even start?

"Landon was always the center of my parents' universe." Laramie swiped at the moisture on her cheeks.

"Other than the farm, life revolved around Landon and his obsession with rodeo."

"That's not true."

She silenced him with an icy glare. "I did extra chores, earned straight A's, babysat, played volleyball, went to church every time the doors were open. Anything I could think of to please my parents. If I wanted something special, I had to earn it, while Landon skipped chores, left a mess all over the house and barely passed his classes. My parents never said a word. Everything was all about what Landon needed or wanted and how they planned to get him to his next competition."

Bitterness had crept into her voice, which made her want to crawl under the table and hide. So humiliating. Who sat around crying about a sibling who got too much attention? Landon was never going to change.

"I should probably know this, but why are you so upset about Landon coming home now?"

"Because he's going to throw a bunch of money at the problem, smile, shake a few hands." She smacked her fist against her palm to punctuate every one of Landon's perceived offenses. "And then, after he signs a zillion autographs, he'll go back to his completely self-absorbed life and I'll have to clean up the mess."

Whoa. A beat of silence filled the space between them. Where did all that come from?

"If I'd known, I wouldn't have sent him that message."

She hugged her knees to her chest. "Go back to your party."

His brow furrowed. "I can't leave you here like this."

"You can't leave Macey and Charlotte with Emily much longer, either."

"Fine, I'll go, but I'm sending Skye back to check on you."

She averted her gaze. "Please, just go away."

Jack hesitated, then stood and strode across the street, back to his friends and family who'd gathered to celebrate his thirtieth birthday.

Laramie sat alone, chin resting on her knees. The woodsy scent of his cologne lingered in the air. She should pull herself together and go back to the party. Today was supposed to be about Jack, after all. But the thought of shoving her anger and her hurt aside and pretending everything was fine provoked a fresh wave of tears. She couldn't pretend her feelings didn't matter. Not anymore.

Chapter Nine

The crowd pressed in, and the scent of hot dogs, popcorn and cotton candy filled the air. It was hot. Really hot. The July sun beat down on the pavement on Main Street, making everything feel ten times hotter. Jack kept his hands locked tightly on the handlebar of the girls' double stroller and craned his neck for a glimpse of Laramie. She'd never come back to the party yesterday, at least not before he left. And he wasn't confident she'd speak to him today, but he had to try. Since his mom was the Fourth of July parade's grand marshal, he expected to run into Gage, Skye, Connor and Drew any minute now. But the only person he really wanted to see was Laramie.

The sunshade protected the twins, and he'd slathered plenty of sunscreen on Macey and Charlotte's pudgy legs when they got out of the truck, but he was still worried the heat would be too much. A rivulet of sweat trickled down his back as he carefully navigated the busy sidewalk. He should probably just go home. Turning the stroller back toward his truck, he spotted Laramie standing on the next street corner. His pulse sped.

In his desperation to reach her, Jack bumped into the person in front of him with the stroller, earning a glare.

"Sorry." He offered an apologetic smile, then stole another glance at Laramie. She looked amazing in a red sundress with skinny straps crisscrossing her bare shoulders. The top emphasized her petite figure and the skirt went to her knees, showing off her tan legs and then her painted red toes in her flip-flops. Okay, so maybe his eyes wandered a little too much.

And she turned and caught him staring. Great. He probably looked like a creep.

His skin flushed hotter as he finally reached her and parked the stroller beside her. "Hey."

"Hey." Laramie's gaze skittered away. Not even a smile. He deserved the frigid greeting, especially after last night, when he'd confessed he invited her brother to his party. Her anger had completely blindsided him. Sending Landon that message had seemed like a great idea at the time. Showed how little he knew about Laramie's feelings. What an idiot.

She reached into her purse, pulled out sunglasses, then slipped them on. Even if Laramie was barely speaking to him, he couldn't think of anyone else he wanted to watch the Fourth of July parade with. Especially since they were running out of time to be together. Only eleven more days until she stopped working as his nanny and took her volleyball team to camp. *Eleven.* How could one small number sound all the alarm bells in his head?

He couldn't think about that right now.

"Do you know which car your mom is riding in?"

"A restored teal-green convertible." Jack scanned the crowd lining the parade route for any sign of his siblings. Plenty of curious gazes from other friends and familiar faces flitted their way. He pretended not to notice.

Charlotte squealed and kicked her bare feet against the frame of the stroller, then flung her plastic toy keys to the ground.

"I don't think she's a fan of being restrained." Laramie bent down and scooped up the keys, then tucked them away in the diaper bag.

Charlotte started crying and kicked harder, then stretched out her arms toward Laramie.

"Charlotte, it's okay." Jack's words did nothing. Macey started to fuss, too.

He released the brake and tried gently rolling the stroller back and forth, but the girls only amped up the tears.

"Want me to hold her?" Laramie offered. "Maybe she'd be happier if she could see the action?"

"I don't want you to have to hold her the whole time. She's super wiggly, and it's so hot."

"I can handle super wiggly. And the heat." Laramie slid the sunshade back. "You're going to have to hold Macey, though."

"All right." Jack wasn't thrilled about letting the girls out of the stroller, but when he looked at Macey squinting at the sun and tears sliding down her flushed cheeks, he relented.

"I packed some hats in the diaper bag yesterday." Laramie pointed with her free hand. "Did you leave them in there?"

He shrugged. Did he?

Without waiting for him to check, Laramie reached inside the diaper bag, then pulled out matching small pink baseball caps and slipped them on the girls' heads.

The tears instantly stopped. Jack stilled. Laramie was so good at this. How was she always prepared with exactly what the babies needed?

Macey looked at him, her eyes wide, as she grasped the bill of the cap with both hands.

"I'm always speechless when I get a new hat, too." Jack held out his arms. "Come here, sweet girl. Let me hold you."

Laramie unclipped the buckles and he lifted Macey from the stroller. Tucking her against his chest, he angled her away from the sun as best as he could. The pink-and-white-striped shirt and matching white shorts were adorable. He'd never been much of a fan of pink until the twins moved into his house. Now he couldn't get enough of the pastels, polka dots and frilly stuff taking over every square inch of extra space.

From the corner of his eye, he watched Laramie balance Charlotte on her hip. The baby had dialed back the fussing as Laramie calmly distracted her with a running commentary about the American flags mounted along Main Street. Warmth spread through Jack's chest. He never could've survived this parade without Laramie.

A muffled percussion beat of a drumline echoed off the storefronts and Macey swiveled in the direction of the sound. The high school marching band began playing somewhere down the street and out of sight, indicating the parade was about to start.

"Do you hear the music?" Jack spoke softly near Macey's ear.

Macey responded with a string of gibberish he couldn't interpret. Other than Skye and Gage's little boy, Connor, he hadn't hung out with many babies. Caring for his daughters exhausted him, but sweet moments like these were slowly shifting his attitude. Being an unexpected father had its rewards.

The cheers and applause grew louder as a classic car came into view, its chrome bumper gleaming and the teal green an eye-catching color that drew comments from people as it passed. Mom sat perched on the back seat, wearing a bright blue blouse and white pants. She had a bouquet of flowers and a fancy ribbon sash. Her smile was radiant, and she waved like she was born to be a parade grand marshal.

We miss you, Dad.

Jack was surprised by how much the emotions overtook him. He hadn't acknowledged missing his father to anyone. Ever. Why now? Swallowing hard against the lump clogging his throat, he focused his attention on Macey.

"See the pretty car?" Laramie asked, pointing.

Mom caught sight of them, smiled wider and blew them a kiss. He was grateful for his sunglasses so no one could see the tears he barely held back. Man, where was all this coming from?

"Oh, let me take a picture real quick." Laramie whipped out her phone and snapped a picture of his mother cruising by.

"The car looks great," Laramie said. "Your mom looks like she belongs there."

"Yeah." Jack barely squeezed out the word.

"Want to take a selfie?"

Before he could answer, Laramie had leaned in close and held her phone at arm's length.

"Wait. Let me take that for you," a woman standing next to them offered.

"Oh." Laramie hesitated, then handed over the phone. "Sure."

Without looking up at him, Laramie slipped her arm around his waist and he shifted Macey to his opposite arm. Charlotte squealed and clapped her hands. Jack rested his hand on Laramie's shoulder, his pulse racing as he realized what was happening. This was everything he'd hoped for—Laramie beside him, celebrating one of his favorite events of the year. The babies were an unexpected bonus.

"You all make a beautiful family." The woman handed Laramie her phone. "What a blessing."

Jack's mouth felt dry as a cotton ball.

"Th-thanks," Laramie mumbled.

Jack glanced at Laramie and tried to gauge her reaction. Since their conversation in the park went sideways and she'd refused to come back to the party, he didn't want to say anything else that might upset her. But the woman's innocent comment stuck with him. *Did* he want a mother for his twins? And could Laramie be the one?

Several hours later, Laramie stood in the church parking lot, savoring the last bite of chocolate sheet cake. After the parade, she'd enjoyed another of her favorite traditions in Merritt's Crossing—the Fourth of July community barbecue. Once she watched the fireworks with Skye, Gage and Connor, her day would be complete.

She tossed her paper plate in the garbage can, then turned in a slow circle. Didn't Skye say they'd meet her right here by the dessert table? Laramie checked the time on her phone. Maybe something had come up with Connor.

"Are you looking for someone?" Jack's voice, low and warm, sent goose bumps skipping across her bare skin. She turned to face him.

"Your sister and her family." Her gaze flitted to the picnic basket and blanket in his arms. "Who are you looking for?"

"You."

Oh. Those beautiful blue eyes searched her face. The hum of conversation and laughter of the kids playing on the playground nearby all faded into the background. For one glorious instant, she stood there, basking in his gaze. She should say something. Anything. *Thank you? Why? It's about time?* How could such simple words get stuck in her throat?

Her phone chimed, defusing the spark humming between them. She forced herself to look away as she pulled her phone from her purse.

Connor is wiped out. We're going home early. Have fun!

She sighed and put her phone away.

"Bad news?"

"Your sister and her family bailed."

Jack grinned. "I guess it's just you and me."

"Where are the twins?"

"I hired a babysitter."

"Who?"

Jack tucked the blanket under one arm, then offered her his other. "Not to worry, Macey and Charlotte are in good hands, and hopefully already asleep. C'mon, the fireworks are about to start."

Laramie blinked, her feet still rooted in place. Who was this version of Jack, hiring a babysitter and showing up with a picnic for two?

"If we're going to claim our spot, we need to go." He angled his head to one side and gently tugged her into motion.

"What spot is that?"

"The place we always sat when we were kids."

She tucked her hand into the crook of his elbow and fell in step beside him, her mind replaying summer nights long ago spent playing freeze tag and kick-the-can and feeling like it took forever before they piled on blankets to watch the fireworks.

A few minutes later, Jack stopped near the trees at the edge of the church's property. He unfolded the quilt, then spread it on a patch of grass with a gentle slope and a fantastic view of the sky over Merritt's Crossing.

"Please, sit down." Jack sank cross-legged on the center of the quilt, patted the space beside him and reached for the basket.

Laramie sat down and tucked her legs beneath her, then smoothed her skirt over her knees. The warm evening air smelled of charcoal and hot dogs and hamburgers. Families gathered nearby, the kids' anticipation for the show almost palpable.

Jack offered her a bottle of water. "Thirsty?"

"Thank you." She twisted off the cap and took a sip.

"I have brownies, pretzels dipped in chocolate and some strawberries." He spread out the dessert options along with two red plates and patriotic napkins printed with stars.

"Wow, you thought of everything." Laramie reached

for the giant pretzel stick with white chocolate and sprinkles on one end. "Did you make this?"

He lifted one shoulder, then reached for a chocolate-covered strawberry.

"I'm very impressed."

He winked. "I wanted tonight to be special."

Her mind raced, analyzing all the details of this very date-like scenario. Had he changed his plans? Declined the job interview? *Stop.* She refused to give voice to the questions. Ignoring the warning signs that everything about her relationship with Jack was about to change, she relaxed and vowed to live in the moment.

"It's perfect." She smiled. "Thank you."

"You're welcome."

Suddenly the night sky filled with pops and fizzes and brilliant shades of green and purple, yellow and orange. Laramie tipped her head back and gasped with each new explosion of color and sound.

Jack slid his arm around her bare shoulders and she looked at him, acutely aware of the warmth of his skin against hers. And those eyes. Drinking her in. She'd waited a long time for Jack to look at her like that. The fireworks soared overhead, casting a silver-blue light across the planes of Jack's face. Her heart hammered as his gaze drifted to her lips. Even if her name appeared in cursive swirls of sparking light right this very second, she couldn't look away.

He inched closer and her breath caught. Then she leaned toward him and closed her eyes. Jack's mouth brushed hers. His lips were soft and warm with a hint of strawberries and chocolate. A shiver of delight raced through her.

Then he deepened the kiss and she responded, pressing her palm against his chest. His fingertips skimmed her jaw as he cupped her cheek in his hand. Her head spun. His touch was firm, yet tender, making her breath shallow. She hadn't felt this way about a kiss in ages. Not even her ex-boyfriend Zeke had made her feel like this.

His kisses had provoked amazing reactions, too. Until he proved she couldn't trust him. And she'd already followed him all the way to Montana. There she was, more than a thousand miles from home and brokenhearted. Panic rising, she pushed against Jack's chest.

She couldn't do this. Not now. And not with Jack. Less than two weeks. That was all she had left. Ten more days with Macey and Charlotte, then she'd leave for volleyball camp and someone else would step into her role. Thinking about it shredded her, but for the sake of her heart, she'd pretend his kisses didn't melt her into a puddle. Pretend she hadn't fallen in love with Jack. Pretend she could live without the twins and Jack in her life.

The sweet taste of Laramie's kiss lingered. He could still feel the softness of her skin under his fingertips, even though she'd scooted across the blanket already.

"I'm sorry." She pressed her hand to her mouth. Was her body still humming from their kiss, too?

"We shouldn't… I mean, that was… That shouldn't have happened."

Jack flinched. So not what he wanted to hear.

She stood quickly and brushed her hands across her skirt. "I'm your nanny, we've been friends for years, and now I—"

"Laramie, please don't."

She started loading the picnic basket. "Don't what?"

"Act like that was a mistake."

She grew still, her bottle of water in hand. "It *was* a mistake, Jack."

He stifled a groan and tipped his head back. He'd made a lot of mistakes in his life, but kissing Laramie was not one of them. The fireworks, the romantic picnic for two, a babysitter for Macey and Charlotte. He thought he'd planned the perfect evening, but based on the way she was avoiding eye contact and packing up like a rabid dog was chasing her, she clearly regretted kissing him.

"I'm supposed to be your friend and here I am leaning in for a kiss and letting you woo me with strawberries and chocolate." The last of the fireworks fizzled and popped in the sky and the silver light gave him a painful glimpse of the confusion on her face. "I mean, you don't even want to live here. I only agreed to help with the girls because you said you were desperate, and now things are going to be all weird."

"All right, all right." He stood and held up both palms, surrendering as she walked their relationship back to the dreaded friend zone. "I get it. Message delivered."

He wasn't sorry they'd kissed, but he couldn't handle her trampling all over his wounded heart with her list of reasons why a relationship would never work. Even though he'd never forget the warmth of her lips against his, or the way it felt to finally hold her in his arms, he'd accept her boundaries, because he hated the thought of losing her friendship.

"C'mon, I'll drive you home." He took the picnic

basket from her. "My truck's parked on the other side of the church."

"I—I'll get a ride with my parents." She glanced around, then reached for her phone. "They're probably still here somewhere."

Ouch. Jack winced. She'd rather ride home with her folks? At least she was honest. While her rejection was like the proverbial salt in a wound, he'd rather know the truth now. She couldn't wait to get away from him and she wasn't interested in a relationship.

"Remember, I'm not coming by tomorrow because I need to help my family finish with harvest." She finally met his gaze. "I'll see you the day after?"

He swallowed hard. "Right. Yeah, see you."

Laramie offered an awkward wave, then turned and worked her way through the crowd lingering on the lawn. He stood there alone, holding the basket and the quilt, and watched her go, hoping she'd turn around. Or even better, come back and tell him she'd—

Jacked huffed out a breath and shook his head as Laramie stopped and spoke to Cooper. He was a fool for even letting himself imagine she'd change her mind. What did he expect her to say? That the kiss was amazing and nothing about tonight was a mistake? She'd start packing tomorrow and look for a job in Utah, too?

Laramie smiled at Cooper, and Jack turned away. She didn't want him. Shocker. He was used to people he cared about not wanting him around.

Laramie was up with the sun, sitting on her back porch with a steaming mug of coffee while Trixie romped around the yard with her puppy. The same one Jack had assured her he wanted, but conveniently hadn't claimed. Honestly the puppy's status was the least of her worries about Jack now.

He'd kissed her.

After all these years of waiting and dreaming and hoping Jack would look at her as anything more than his sister's best friend, he'd finally kissed her.

And she'd kissed him back.

Even though she'd declared their first kiss a mistake, her heart blip-blipped into a spontaneous two-step as her mind replayed every delicious detail. She'd enjoyed the sensation of Jack's lips on hers. And that was a problem. Jack didn't want to stay in Merritt's Crossing, and she couldn't possibly leave. Not now. Not when her grandfather's dementia was progressing, and her family hadn't found an affordable place for him to live.

Trixie dropped a cloth Frisbee at her feet and backed up, her tail wagging, as she waited for Laramie to start another round of fetch. Laramie put her mug down on the side table and then flung the Frisbee across the yard. Trixie and the puppy raced away, barking. Dew glistened on the grass and the sun cast its early-morning rays through the trees lining her back fence.

What would Macey and Charlotte think about the dogs? They were a little young now, but having pets could be fun for them once they were able to run around in the yard. Except they'd be more than eight hours away in Utah. A hollow ache filled Laramie's chest at the thought of not being with them anymore. She couldn't fathom all the ways they'd grow and change over the next several months. By the time Jack came back for a visit, the twins would probably both be walking.

Even though she'd grown attached to the baby girls, she couldn't trust her heart to Jack when she'd seen the outcome of his impulsive behavior. Sure, the girls were a blessing, but he was still so wounded and broken over the loss of his father and uncle. His fear of commitment was intense, and it terrified her. If she followed him to Utah and he decided he couldn't handle a serious relationship, she'd be stuck in an unfamiliar place, nursing a broken heart. Again. And those sweet babies didn't deserve to be caught in the middle. They'd been through so much already.

Trixie returned and dropped the Frisbee on the deck. Her pink tongue lolling, she pranced around, anticipating Laramie's next throw. The puppy nipped at his mother's heels and scampered in circles.

Laramie chuckled. "I have time for one more throw."

She tossed the toy again, then stood and reached for her coffee. Today was supposed to be the last day of wheat harvest and she'd promised her parents and her grandmother she'd help feed the workers lunch and dinner.

A few minutes later, she'd settled the dogs with plenty of food and water, tucked her ponytail in a baseball cap, then quickly fixed another cup of coffee to go. She faced a long day ahead and the lack of sleep after an emotional evening weighed her down. Massaging the knotted muscles in her neck and shoulders provided little relief, but she wasn't about to back out on her family during their busiest season of the year.

Laramie got in her car, tucked her phone and her insulated mug in the cupholders, then drove toward the farm. Her thoughts drifted to Jack and the twins. How did he plan to spend the day? Had he hired another babysitter again or was he on his own?

Stop. She battled back the mental images of Jack smiling as he sat on his living room floor with Charlotte and Macey babbling while they gnawed on their favorite toys. Laramie jabbed at the button on her console and quickly selected a radio station. It wasn't her favorite song, but the upbeat tempo and lyrics might distract her.

Her phone buzzed with an incoming call. Laramie's breath caught. She hoped it was Jack. Instead, her brother's name and number filled the screen.

"No, thank you." She turned the radio up louder. "It's dangerous to talk and drive."

Guilt twisted her insides. Answering her phone while driving wasn't illegal, but her students weren't allowed to, and she lectured them on the dangers of distracted driving all the time. Wasn't she supposed to set a positive example?

Except she had the capability to answer his call hands-free. And intentionally avoiding Landon wasn't right, either.

He'd made a point of speaking to her after the parade and she'd hugged him, but part of her still hoped he'd gone back to Texas or Oklahoma or wherever bull riding took him next. Because if Landon hung around long enough, he'd convince her parents to make a questionable decision.

When Laramie turned down the long dirt driveway toward her family's farm, sunlight glinted off the chrome bumper of Landon's large white pickup parked in front of the farmhouse.

She groaned. "Seriously?"

Lord, please help me to be patient and loving. He is my brother, after all.

Another wave of guilt crested as she parked her car next to Landon's truck. Prayer hadn't been a priority in her life lately. Too busy trying to help everyone and force circumstances to bend to her will.

She sighed, grabbed her phone and her coffee, and then exited the car.

"Good morning." The storm door slammed behind him as Landon came out of the house.

"Hey." Laramie met him at the bottom of the wide porch steps. "I didn't realize you were still here."

Landon's sleepy smile dimmed. "You can't get rid of me that easy, sis."

"Are you driving the combine?"

"Yep." Landon wore faded jeans and an old Merritt's Crossing High School Basketball T-shirt, and his damp blond hair curled around his ears. He held a water bottle and a baseball cap in his hands. Laramie scanned his face, noting the fatigue etching his features.

"I'm sure Dad needs you to get started, but maybe at lunch we could talk about Grandpa?" Laramie lowered her voice. "He needs to move to a memory care facility, but the closest place with availability is in Denver, and it's too expensive."

Landon palmed the back of his neck. "I wish I could help."

"That sounds like you can't." She tried not to sound aggravated. Wasn't he a champion bull rider? "What happened to all the prize money you've won?"

He hesitated, avoiding her gaze as he carved the toe of his boot through the dirt. "I'm broke."

Of course he was. Her parents had put everything into her brother, and he'd squandered it. Another affirmation that she couldn't trust men to be responsible.

A day without Laramie moved slower than a traffic jam on the interstate.

Everywhere he turned in his house, from the baby

clothes neatly stacked in the girls' dresser drawers to the pots and pans arranged in his kitchen cabinets, reminders of her infiltrated his thoughts. Her absence prompted a restlessness he couldn't shake.

Jack sighed and flopped on the sofa. Macey and Charlotte were in the middle of a long afternoon nap. He'd tossed another load of laundry in the washer, defrosted some chicken for dinner and picked up the toys off the floor. The minutes crept by. He grabbed the remote control, turned on the TV and wandered through the channels. Not that he'd be able to focus on a show. His mind promptly circled back to Laramie and the kiss they'd shared during the fireworks.

He flung his arm over his eyes, determined to block out the barrage of images that memory provoked. The smoothness of her cheek against his fingertips, the sweet taste of her soft lips moving against his. Her touch had silenced his doubts. Snuffed out the worry about his future and made him believe, just for a second, that he could do anything. Even stay in Merritt's Crossing if that meant building a life with her.

Then she'd trampled his hopes when she'd panicked and pushed him away.

She'd rejected him. The truth slammed into him again, like a hammer smashing his thumb when he'd missed hitting a nail.

His phone pinged and he sat up, grateful for a distraction. Part of him hoped the text was from her. He traded the remote for his phone and scanned the group text message. An ache settled in his gut. Laramie wasn't involved in Emily's last-minute plans for a cookout. While Jack noted Cooper's name and a handful of other friends included in the invitation, he wasn't interested. He dropped the phone on the cushion without responding.

He didn't want to take the girls out with his friends. None of them had kids yet. Talk about awkward. They'd get to sit around on Emily's deck and relax, while he'd wear himself out keeping Macey and Charlotte happy. Besides, someone would likely ask about him and Laramie and he'd have to sidestep their questions. No, thank you.

Back in the day, he would've been the first to show up at a spontaneous get-together and probably the last to leave. Not tonight. He had to think about what was best for Macey and Charlotte. And selfishly, he needed to shield his wounded heart.

Determined to spend the last few minutes of the girls' nap time on something productive, he reached for his phone again. The woman who'd looked after the girls while he'd gone to the Fourth of July festival had offered to babysit anytime. She seemed confident and content managing twins. While she didn't put the dishes away or fold any laundry, Jack was impressed with her immediate warmth and attentiveness toward Macey and Charlotte.

He needed to find reliable childcare. Quickly. Laramie had to leave for volleyball camp soon. Too soon. Dread pitted his stomach. He pushed the feeling aside, sent the woman a message inquiring about her availability, then started the next episode of a home renovation show.

Laramie didn't want him, so it was time to move on.

Chapter Ten

The next morning, Laramie washed the bottles, plastic spoons and bowls from breakfast, then set them in the drying rack on Jack's kitchen counter. The muffled sound of Jack's voice on the phone in his office sent anxiety rippling through her. Not that she didn't enjoy having him close by. That was the problem. She enjoyed being around him too much. And it was all coming to an end. The snippets of conversation filtering into the room hinted he was interviewing for a job.

She left the kitchen, searching for another task or chore to complete while Macey and Charlotte napped. Eavesdropping was wrong. What Jack did with his life was really none of her business. She was the one who'd declared their kiss a mistake. And she'd told him from the beginning that he was foolish for moving away, especially now that he had two children to consider.

But it sounded like Jack wasn't interested in listening to her advice.

He'd made his decision and now they were at a stalemate. She wasn't uprooting her entire life to move to Utah. No matter how much she cared about Macey,

Charlotte and Jack. Or how often she thought about that kiss. Her skin tingled with the memory of Jack's touch. But kissing him had been a lousy, impulsive choice, and that was the kind of behavior that only led to heartache.

She approached the unfolded laundry sitting in Jack's living room. All she had to do was stay focused on caring for Macey and Charlotte for eight more days and then they'd be at the end of their agreement. He'd have to find a new nanny because she was taking her team to volleyball camp. Her stomach cinched in a tighter knot. For the first time in ten years, she wasn't looking forward to going to camp. The bonding, camaraderie, friendly competition against other teams—even the boisterous atmosphere in the van on the drive to the university— usually made the trip the highlight of her summer.

Until she started spending her days holding the world's cutest babies. She sat down on the sofa and plucked a white onesie with navy-blue stars from the pile of clean laundry. She held it up. Baby girl clothes were so adorable. She folded the onesie and set it on the coffee table, trying hard not to think about how domestic this whole scenario was. Jack at work in his home office, the babies taking their morning naps, a pile of clean clothes to fold while the sweet scent of fabric softener enveloped her.

Her phone rang, rescuing her from the painful realization that her days playing house with Jack were numbered. She pulled her phone from her jeans pocket. Grandma's name and number filled the screen.

Oh no. Laramie's heart raced as she accepted the call. "Grandma?"

"Hi, sweetie." Grandma sounded stressed.

"Everything okay?"

"Not exactly. I have a doctor's appointment in Limon at eleven o'clock. Landon said he'd stay with your grandfather, but he isn't here yet."

Shocker. Laramie squeezed her eyes shut. "Do you need me to come and stay with him?"

"Well, I need somebody. If I don't leave soon, I'm going to be late."

Laramie glanced over her shoulder toward Jack's office. The twins would probably wake up soon. Jack mentioned earlier he had a lot going on with work and spending an hour in an interview was putting him behind. If she left for a couple of hours, he'd struggle to feed the girls their lunch and get his work done.

"Laramie, are you still there?"

"Yes, Grandma. I'm here." She strode toward the door. "I'll be there in a few minutes."

"Oh, good." Grandma sighed. "I called your mom, but she didn't answer."

"She mentioned she was going to Denver today." Laramie fumbled in her purse for her keys. "Dad's probably out in the field somewhere on the tractor."

"I called him, but he didn't answer, either."

"Okay, let me hang up so I can drive. I'll see you soon."

"Thank you, hon. I don't know what I'd do without you."

Me, either. Laramie ended the call. She hesitated beside her car and quickly texted Jack an explanation. Guilt knifed at her as she hit Send. Abandoning her post felt so traitorous. She'd never leave school in the middle of the day without permission from her principal.

But this was different. Her family needed her. And

she wasn't leaving the twins unsupervised. They were both still asleep and Jack could handle the babies on his own this afternoon. He was their father, after all. Situations like this emphasized the reasons why she couldn't move away. She couldn't stand the thought of being several hours from home knowing her grandparents didn't have the kind of help they needed. After all, if she wasn't here, who would her grandmother rely on?

The crying grew louder.

Jack narrowed his gaze and tried to focus on the data filling his computer screen. His stomach growled, reminding him that he'd worked through lunch, but he just needed a few more minutes before he could take a break.

Except Macey and Charlotte were making it extremely difficult to focus. He raked his hand through his hair and scanned the update from his project manager again. Laramie was probably fixing the bottles before she changed their diapers. In the past few weeks, Laramie had established a process for caring for the girls. And he wasn't about to question or criticize. He certainly didn't have a better approach. Except it seemed like the babies had been crying for longer than normal.

The muffled sound of someone knocking pulled his attention from his computer.

His brain was still humming from the phone interview he'd finished earlier. The job in Utah offered everything he was looking for.

The crying coming from the twins' bedroom echoed through the whole house.

He'd meant to check in with Laramie after his interview, but one of his project managers had called and pulled him into a long conversation about an issue with a client in Kansas City.

The knocking grew louder while Macey and Charlotte kept crying. Man, what was going on with Laramie? She never let the babies cry this long. Jack pushed back his chair and stood, massaging his forehead with his fingertips. The dull pain that had started a few minutes ago was morphing into an intense headache.

He grabbed his phone from his desk as he crossed his office. Two missed texts. The first was from Miranda, the social worker who'd brought Macey and Charlotte to him. She'd sent a message forty-five minutes ago, stating she was in the area and planned to stop by. His heart hammered. Was that who it was at the door?

Jack strode into the kitchen. "Laramie?"

She didn't answer. And the twins were not in their high chairs waiting for their lunch like he'd expected. Jack craned his neck to see out the window over the sink. Laramie's car was gone, and Miranda's SUV was parked in his driveway.

Panic welled. Macey and Charlotte were wailing now. This time the doorbell rang. Miranda could probably hear the crying. She must think he was completely inept.

Jack glanced at the next message on his phone. It was from Laramie.

My grandparents are having an emergency. Hopefully I'll be back later. Sorry.

"Hopefully you'll be back later?" Jack scoffed and tossed his phone onto the counter. He hated that her grandparents were struggling, but she was supposed to be helping him. They had an agreement. She couldn't just run off and leave. How long had she been gone, anyway?

He reached over and turned off the volume on the baby monitor. Macey and Charlotte's cries still echoed through the whole house, but at least they weren't amplified through the speaker on the kitchen counter.

Jack was paralyzed with indecision. Answer the door and invite Miranda into this chaos? Then she'd have a front row seat to his inability to care for the girls on his own. Or should he pick the twins up and comfort them, then answer the door so it at least looked like he was trying?

The crying was too much. He couldn't handle answering the door while the twins sobbed in their room, alone.

"Hang on a second!" He called over his shoulder, then jogged back down the hall to the girls' bedroom. He pushed open the door. Macey and Charlotte sat beside each other, sobbing, their little hands gripping the rails of their new crib.

"Oh no." Jack's chest ached at their flushed faces and the tears glistening on their cheeks. "Shhh, it's okay. Daddy's here now."

He carefully picked Macey up and then Charlotte. Their diapers had leaked through their outfits. He quickly glanced around their room. No diapers. Seriously? His pulse sped. He'd figure out what to do about that in a few minutes. He couldn't keep Miranda waiting on the porch much longer.

The babies kept crying as he strode through the house, nearly tripping over a discarded toy in the living room. Why couldn't Laramie have picked another day to rescue her grandparents? He needed her here. Now.

Somehow, he managed to force a smile and open the

door while holding Macey and Charlotte. "Hi, Miranda. Sorry to keep you waiting."

"Hello, Jack." Miranda's expression softened as her gaze flitted between the babies. "How are your girls doing?"

He hesitated. "I know it looks and smells pretty bad, but things aren't always like this."

"Oh?"

"My nanny, Laramie, is usually here. She had to deal with a family emergency, so I'm flying solo." He raised his voice to be heard over the crying but that only made Charlotte and Macey cry louder. Man, this was getting worse by the second.

"May I come in?" Miranda shifted her bag to the other shoulder. "I'd be glad to hold one of the babies while you catch your breath."

"Uh, sure." Sweat dampened his skin and his head felt like it might explode. He stepped back to let Miranda inside, then carefully passed Charlotte to her. "I'm sorry, she smells terrible. I'm, uh, trying to do something about that."

"Come here, sweetheart." Miranda gently braced Charlotte against her shoulder. "Shhh, it's going to be all right."

Was it? Jack wished he had a fraction of Miranda's confidence. And did that mean she wasn't alarmed by the chaos unfolding in his home?

C'mon, Laramie. I need you. He couldn't handle a diaper crisis and lunch with Miranda hovering over his shoulder. She'd figure out in about two seconds that he shouldn't be responsible for two babies. Fear latched icy tentacles around his heart. What would happen to Charlotte and Macey if he was deemed unfit to parent?

* * *

Laramie parked in front of Jack's house, grabbed her purse then exited her car. What a day. Grandma's appointment had taken much longer than expected and Landon never had showed up. She'd enjoyed spending time with her Grandpa, especially since he was having a good day.

Except Jack had texted her three times asking when she'd be back. Her flip-flops slapped against her feet as she hurried toward his porch. Jack was clearly annoyed. And she'd felt bad for leaving him with the girls when he was trying to work. Until her grandfather had taken a fall, scaring her half to death and confirming she'd made the right decision to stay with him.

Thankfully, he'd only cut his forehead. She'd left him resting comfortably with her grandmother, then texted her parents and told them what happened. They needed to find a safer place for Grandpa to live as soon as possible.

She stepped inside and quietly closed the door. The sound of a baby toy playing a nursery rhyme and the girls babbling greeted her. Laramie hesitated, then kicked off her flip-flops and walked into Jack's living room.

He sat on the sofa, his computer on his lap, fingers clicking over the keys. His lips were pressed into a flat line and he didn't speak to her.

All righty, then.

Charlotte sat near Jack's feet, pressing the button that played the familiar tune on repeat. Macey was riding in the baby swing by the window and she squealed when she saw Laramie.

"Hey, everybody." Laramie forced a smile and injected enthusiasm into her voice. "How's it going?"

"Fine." Jack didn't bother to look up. "Nice of you to join us."

Ouch. She fidgeted with the buckle on her purse. "I had to help my grandparents. They were having an emergency."

A muscle in his jaw twitched.

Boy, he was oozing empathy.

Charlotte crawled toward her. "Buh-buh-buh."

Laramie bit back a snide comment and focused on Charlotte. "Hi, cutie pie. What are you playing with?"

The baby offered a slobbery grin, then stretched her arms high. Laramie's heart squeezed. At least someone around here was happy to see her. She scooped Charlotte into her arms and pressed a kiss to her chubby cheek.

"Miranda made a surprise visit." Jack raked his fingers through his hair. "Thankfully, she didn't revoke my parental rights."

Laramie froze. "I didn't know a social worker had that kind of power."

Jack glared at her. "The girls were crying for a long time because I didn't know you weren't here. When Miranda came in, Charlotte and Macey had dirty diapers, they wouldn't stop crying and they were beyond hungry. I looked totally incompetent."

Oh no. She swallowed hard. "I—I'm sorry. I thought you'd be fine for an hour or two."

"Yeah, well, I wasn't. *We* weren't." Jack shifted his attention back to his computer. "I couldn't find another babysitter on short notice. You were gone for four hours, by the way."

Like a bolt of lightning striking the fields outside, his words sent anger zinging through her. Laramie breathed deep, hoping the lingering scent of Charlotte's baby shampoo might help her calm down. Why was he being so feisty? "I guess you'll have to dock my pay."

Rat-a-tat-tat. Did he always take out his frustration on his keyboard? "A conversation before you left would've been helpful."

"I didn't have the luxury of a conversation, Jack. You were on the phone and my grandmother needed me."

"Here's the thing—I needed you. The girls needed you." His icy gaze bore into her. "We had an agreement, Laramie."

"I said I was sorry." She perched Charlotte on her other hip and met his gaze. "And by the way, I do believe I rearranged my entire life to help you out. A little gratitude would be nice."

He stared at her, disbelief flashing across his features. "Thanks. Thanks for everything. You've made it clear where your priorities lie."

"You don't sound grateful. And what do you mean by my priorities?" Her voice was getting dangerously close to yelling. Macey and Charlotte were giving her wide-eyed stares, but she wasn't going to let him shame her for doing the right thing. "Why are you so mad that I chose to help my elderly grandparents and left you home alone with *your own children*?"

"Because you always choose your family." He set his laptop down and stood. "I'm going to the store. We're out of diapers." He brushed past her, grabbed his keys and left, slamming the door behind him.

Hot tears pricked her eyelids. She stared after him, while Charlotte fussed and gnawed on her fist. How could he be so self-absorbed? And why was she so surprised that he'd reverted to his same old juvenile behavior—leaving when conflict arrived?

Chapter Eleven

Today was the day. He couldn't avoid it any longer. Jack stood in his backyard, hands on his hips, and stared at the woodshop's closed door. While the girls napped, he was going to sort through Dad and Uncle Kenny's tools.

The relentless afternoon sun heated his skin. The harsh words he'd said in his final exchange with Dad echoed in his head. Words he could never take back.

I'm nothing like you and I never want to be!

His father had died thinking Jack was ashamed of the family business, but nothing could be further from the truth.

Some of his best memories had happened in this shed. Jack had hung out with Uncle Kenny and Dad whenever he could. The old radio in the corner played classic rock music while his uncle and his father both sang off-key. Uncle Kenny never passed up an opportunity to tell a corny joke, and the man was a master when it came to turning slabs of wood into furniture.

From his father and his uncle, Jack had learned the value of making something practical with his hands.

Uncle Kenny took great pride in his work, knowing a table or a dresser he'd made might stay in a family for generations.

But then Uncle Kenny had accused Dad of ripping him off, which Jack's father denied, and they'd stopped speaking. It wasn't long before the unthinkable happened, leaving Aunt Willa to raise a rebellious, teenage McKenna by herself. That was when Jack had decided he wanted nothing to do with a business that decimated their family.

Bracing for the hurt, Jack forced himself to approach the building. He glanced at the portable baby monitor clipped to his jeans. Maybe the girls would wake up and save him from this painful trip down memory lane.

Nope. Macey and Charlotte were both sound asleep. Besides, he'd asked Drew to help him pack up the tools and figure out what to sell. And what to keep, if anything. Jack hesitated, then unlocked the door and pushed it open. The familiar scent of sawdust mixed with varnish filled his senses and unleashed an onslaught of more memories. His father's hands, strong and calloused, teaching him to use the level, and his uncle's tender care after Jack pinched his finger in a vise grip.

Sucking in a breath, he reached in and flipped the light switch. The bare bulbs hanging over Uncle Kenny's workbench flickered on, illuminating a partially finished dining table. Emotion tightened Jack's throat. Had they really abandoned his uncle's last project? He ran his hands over the smoothly sanded surface. What a shame. He stepped farther inside and surveyed the rest of the woodshop's contents. Tools, hunks of wood, the old dust-covered radio. An empty soda can on a step stool. If Jack didn't know any better, he'd think Uncle

Kenny or his father were coming right back. Sadly, that wasn't the case. He'd lost them both all too soon.

And it had been his fault his father had died. Guilt and grief crashed into him as the memory of their last day together flashed before his eyes. The devastated look on his father's face before Jack stomped out.

A car door slammed and pulled Jack from his stupor. Wiping a tear, he turned and glanced toward the house. Drew strode toward him in his deputy sheriff's uniform. His steps faltered when he saw Jack standing inside.

"Whoa." Drew's eyes widened. "You said you wanted to clean out the place, but I didn't think you meant it."

Jack bristled at his brother's comment. "This is good stuff. Somebody could use the tools. Better than letting everything rust."

Drew was silent. Jack waited for the inevitable comment about how he was that somebody. Instead, Drew rattled the ice in his to-go cup, then took a long sip.

Jack tugged his phone from his pocket and opened an app on his phone. He'd make a list of all the tools, then research online for the resale value.

"How was your holiday?" Drew ran his hand along the arm of a rocking chair. "Enjoy the fireworks?"

Jack winced at the double meaning threaded through his brother's words and examined one of the chisels on the workbench.

"Uh-oh." Drew studied him. "What happened?"

"We had a great time at the parade and the fireworks were incredible." Thoughts of the kiss he'd shared with Laramie resurfaced. Again. "Until she said kissing me was a mistake and left with her parents."

He left out the part about the harsh words they'd exchanged when she'd come back from helping her grandparents. He wasn't interested in his brother's unsolicited advice about that, either. Drew's radio crackled and he paused to listen, then adjusted the volume.

"I know, I know." Jack set the chisel down and took a picture with his phone. "You don't have to say it."

"Say what?"

"That Laramie will never fall in love with a guy like me and I was stupid to even try."

"I didn't—"

"I should've taken over the furniture business like Dad wanted me to. Then we wouldn't have had a huge fight before he died. Maybe—"

"Wait. What?"

"You don't have to pretend." Jack shoved his phone back in his pocket, then glared at Drew. "I take full responsibility for our nasty confrontation. It's no secret that you all blame me for his death."

Drew rubbed his fingers along his jaw and stared at Jack. "There's so much wrong with what you just said that I don't even know where to begin."

Jack's scalp prickled. "What's that supposed to mean?"

"Look, knock it off with the whole victim thing. Nobody blames you for anything. We're all getting on with our lives, including Mom and Aunt Willa. McKenna is almost finished with college, and Connor has two parents who love him. Stop letting your regrets about the past hold you hostage."

"My past isn't holding me hostage."

"Really." Drew's gaze narrowed. "Is that why you're giving up?"

Jack crossed his arms over his chest. "I'm not giving up."

"You're cleaning out the shop even though you probably have more talent for woodworking in one arm than our father ever had. Now you're telling me you finally kissed Laramie but that didn't go like you'd hoped, so you're not going to pursue a relationship, and last I heard, you're planning on leaving town." Drew shrugged. "Sounds to me like you're giving up and running away, bro."

"Or maybe there's no reason for me to stay."

"Ouch. Thanks a lot." Drew shook his head in disbelief. "Why don't you tell me how you really feel about your family?" His radio crackled again and he turned and walked away. "I've got to get back to work."

"Thanks for stopping by," Jack called after him, not even trying to keep the sarcasm from his tone. The last thing he needed or wanted was a pep talk from his older brother. Especially since Drew didn't know what he was talking about. Jack had finally taken responsibility for his actions, and his family *still* thought he was wrong. Didn't he get any credit for trying to be a decent father for Macey and Charlotte?

"I'm *not* acting like a victim," Jack grumbled. Or was he?

Raking his hand through his hair, he surveyed the woodshop one more time. The tools, equipment and partially completed projects filled every square inch of space. Overwhelmed, he left and slammed the door. He'd underestimated how much effort it would take to sort through years of possessions. His conversation with Drew had zapped all his optimism anyway.

Jack stomped toward the house, kicking pebbles out of his path. Let his family think what they wanted. He was tired of trying to prove them wrong. A new start in another state was exactly what he and his daughters needed.

* * *

Bleary-eyed, Laramie sidestepped Trixie and Jack's puppy, whom she'd named Bear. Unofficially, of course. Even though he hadn't said a word about taking possession of the adorable animal, he'd paid for him. She'd grown tired of referring to the dog as puppy. Bear danced around her on his humongous feet while she poured dog food into both bowls.

On her way to the sink to get their water, she jabbed at the power button on her coffee maker. Morning sunlight filtered through her kitchen window above the sink and she squinted. Once Trixie and Bear were satisfied, Laramie leaned against the kitchen counter and rolled her neck in a slow circle, wincing at the ache still lingering in her upper arms and shoulders. Wheat harvest was a marathon of filling coolers with water, hauling them out to the workers in the field, then hurrying back to the house to help serve lunch and dinner.

While she was glad the grueling work was over and thankful for a successful harvest, now she had to face a new reality—less than a week left working for Jack. Maybe he'd stay tucked away in his office while she took care of Macey and Charlotte. Except the twins consistently napped twice, which meant plenty of time for Jack to linger.

Or what if she and Jack both pretended the kiss hadn't changed anything? That they hadn't had a tense conversation about her always choosing her family?

Laramie sighed. She'd have a hard time pulling that off. How was she supposed to spend the next five days in his house, smelling that outdoorsy cologne, and trying not to stare at his angular jaw? Or those hands that had caressed her cheek? And how could she look into those gorgeous eyes and not think about the incredible kiss they'd shared?

She took her favorite chipped green mug from the cabinet and filled it with coffee. The robust fragrance wafted toward her and she quickly grabbed the carton of half-and-half from the fridge. She needed coffee to clear the sleepy fog from her brain so she could formulate an emergency action plan.

Taking Charlotte and Macey out of Jack's house was an option, but it required a lot of energy and patience, two commodities in short supply today. Unless she had a sidekick. Laramie stirred cream and sugar into her coffee with one hand and scrolled through her contacts in her phone with the other. Who did she know that might want to spend an hour or so hanging out with her and two adorable baby girls?

The farm was always an option, although her parents were exhausted, and she didn't want to spend any more time with Landon than she already had. His confession that he didn't have any money made her so mad she didn't trust herself not to say something she'd regret later.

Laramie scrolled past Skye's number, hesitated, then scrolled back. Gage and Skye had closed the furniture store for a few days to give themselves a break and honor the holiday. Macey and Charlotte weren't much fun for Connor to hang out with, but Skye might meet them at the park since it was across the street from their house. Then if Connor got bored, Skye could take him home.

She dropped two slices of bread in the toaster, then sent Skye a text about a park playdate. A few minutes later, Laramie was spreading peanut butter on her toast when Skye responded.

I wish I could. Gage is working and I'm so sick I can barely get out of bed. Is now a good time to mention I'm pregnant?

Laramie squealed so loud that the dogs barked. She stabbed the knife into the peanut butter container and quickly called Skye.

"Hello?" Skye's voice was barely above a whisper.

"Congratulations!"

"Good morning to you, too." Skye cleared her throat. "And thank you."

"That's so exciting. I'm really happy for you." Laramie reached for her coffee. "When are you due?"

"I'm not sure. Maybe February? My doctor's appointment is scheduled for next week."

"Gage must be thrilled."

"You have no idea."

Laramie chuckled. "Have you told your family yet?"

"My mom knows. I'm planning to tell my brothers today. I'll call Jack before you go over there."

"That's kind of why I'm calling."

"Hang on." Skye's voice was muffled as she gave Connor some instructions. "Sorry. He wants breakfast and I need a minute, so I'm letting him watch another show. Don't judge."

Laramie sipped her coffee. "No judgment here."

"What were we talking about?" Skye asked. "Oh, right. Jack. What's going on?"

"I kissed him."

"It's about time."

"No, it's all wrong. The timing. Jack. All of it." Laramie padded into the living room and curled up in the recliner with her coffee. Trixie settled at her feet while Bear wrestled with a stuffed cheeseburger.

"But I thought this is what you wanted?" Fatigue laced Skye's words. "You've been attracted to Jack for—hold on. Connor, wait."

Laramie winced. If Skye was struggling with morning sickness and home alone with Connor, she should offer to help, not monopolize her time on the phone, rehashing one silly kiss.

"Sorry." Skye returned to the conversation. "Are Macey and Charlotte holding you back? I totally get that. Dating a single parent definitely has its challenges."

"No, the twins are adorable." Laramie smiled just thinking about the babies and their distinct personalities, and the warmth that exploded in her chest when she plastered kisses on their chubby cheeks.

"Then what are you afraid of?"

"I told him our kiss was a mistake."

"Oh."

"I can't go back now and tell him I didn't mean it. By the way, the kiss was pretty great." Nervous laughter escaped. "Sorry, I know that's not what you want to hear about your brother."

"You're avoiding the question." Skye's voice was flat.

"What? No, I'm not."

"Yes, you are. I asked what you're afraid of."

Doubt niggled its way in. She didn't want to peer into that vulnerable, broken place left empty by Zeke's rejection.

"Laramie? Still with me?"

"Yeah," she sighed. "If I'm honest, I'm afraid he'll break my heart."

There. The absolute truth. Laramie set her coffee on the side table, then stood and paced.

"I don't blame you for being cautious," Skye said gently. "Jack has a history of being reckless and impulsive. It will take a special woman to ground him, even more than the twins already have. You can be that person, Laramie. I know you can."

"If Zeke hadn't cheated on me when I followed him to Montana, I might be brave enough to try and follow Jack wherever he and the babies wanted to go." Laramie swallowed hard. "But I can't go through that kind of pain again. Can't take that risk right now. My family, my work, everything that matters to me is right here."

"Not everything," Skye said. "If Jack and the twins move away, will you be able to live with the hole that's left in your life?"

Skye's question stung, like an icy snowball hurled at her when she wasn't looking. She was so focused on guarding her heart and staying close to her family that she hadn't considered what her life would be like without Jack, Macey and Charlotte. That mental image created hurt, too.

"I really want a husband and children," Laramie admitted. "And every day, week and month that passes by, I wonder if that will ever happen for me."

"I understand."

"I want to believe Jack has changed since he's become a father. Saying goodbye to Macey and Charlotte will break my heart if they move away, but I'm afraid to follow him. And not only that, but he always runs from conflict. He'd feel much better emotionally if he stuck around and worked through his issues."

"Then why don't you ask him to stay?"

"Because I want him to love me enough that I don't have to ask him." Laramie squeezed her eyes shut as shame twisted her stomach in a knot. "Is that pathetic or what?"

"No, it's not," Skye said. "What are you going to do next?"

"If you'll let me, I'd like to borrow Connor for a few hours."

Skye chuckled. "You're a glutton for punishment."

"We need a distraction. A buffer. Someone to hang out with us today."

"Connor will definitely keep you distracted," Skye said. "Come on over. I'll have him ready to go when you get here."

Laramie ended the call, then quickly drank the rest of her coffee. Skye's questions percolated in her head while she showered and dressed. Had she made the right choice—telling Jack their kiss was a mistake? He was charming and funny and incredibly handsome. But she couldn't shake the ominous feeling that transplanting her life in a new city eight hours away was a risk she couldn't afford. No matter how much he'd changed, if Jack bailed on her, she'd rather face that rejection surrounded by family and friends than in a strange place where she had no one. Just like the last time.

Jack tugged the roll of packing tape across the cardboard box, sealing it closed.

Charlotte bounced up and down inside the baby swing he'd suspended from the shed's door frame, while

Macey sat inside the portable crib, gnawing on a vinyl book. With the window air-conditioning unit blasting and the woodshop's garage-style door rolled open, he'd managed to make the place tolerable for them.

Sweat dampened his brow and Jack swiped his forehead with the hem of his T-shirt, then slid the cardboard box against the wall next to the other two he'd already packed. He grabbed a permanent marker from his jeans pocket, then wrote Magazines and Manuals on the outside of the box. His dad and his uncle apparently never threw anything away, based on all the stuff Jack had discovered when he opened the cabinets along the back wall.

Jack set the tape down and checked the time on his phone. Skye had called a few minutes ago and announced her pregnancy. Then Laramie had texted that she was bringing Connor along for a couple of hours so Skye could rest. He probably needed to take a break from packing another box. Connor was going to need his undivided attention, and the shed wasn't a safe place for a three-year-old to hang out. A car door slammed, then Laramie and Connor's voices filled the air.

Charlotte gnawed on her finger and swiveled in the direction of the noise.

"Hold on, ladies." Jack quickly stowed the more dangerous tools that were spread out on the workbench and prepared for the imminent arrival of his nephew. "Here comes Connor."

Gravel crunched under Connor's shoes as he barreled toward the shed in a red T-shirt and gray shorts. He stopped and pointed toward his feet. "Wook! New shoes."

Jack smiled. Connor's inability to pronounce his L's was adorable. "Nice. Do they make you run fast?"

"Yup. Watch." Connor tucked his tongue in the corner of his mouth then took off running around the yard, his little legs and arms pumping. Charlotte squealed and bounced up and down in her swing. Jack rubbed at the tightness in his chest. If he moved, the twins would miss out on a lot of time with their cousin. And Skye and Gage's new baby.

He was making the right decision, though. Wasn't he?

"Good morning." Laramie strode toward him carrying an insulated mug. Jack's pulse sped. He'd missed her. Was this going to be weird now that they'd kissed? And argued about her helping her grandmother? Hopefully not. She'd been a good friend to him, and he hated that they'd wrecked their effortless camaraderie.

Laramie's long hair gleamed in the sunshine and she wore a pink T-shirt and khaki shorts. The flowery fragrance that had become so familiar drifted toward him as she stepped inside the shed.

"Hey." His mouth was as dry as the sawdust that still coated most of the shed's cement floor.

She glanced around and her smooth brow furrowed. "Are you packing?"

He nodded. "It's time to clean this place out."

Laramie trapped her lip behind her teeth and Jack tried not to let his gaze linger on her mouth. Or think about how soft and warm her lips had felt against his.

Macey cried and pressed her face to the mesh panel on the side of the portable crib.

Jack checked the time on his phone. "They're probably ready for naps."

"I'll take the girls inside." Laramie moved toward Macey. "Come here, pumpkin."

"I can keep an eye on Connor," Jack said.

"Oh, right." Laramie wedged Macey on her hip, then flashed him an apologetic look. "Thanks for letting me bring him along today. I felt so bad for Skye. She's super sick."

"He's always welcome here, you know that."

"Hop, hop, hop." Connor's eyes gleamed as he bounced into the shed. "I'm a bunny."

"You're a good hopper." Laramie tousled his hair. "Stay here and play with your uncle Jack while I put the babies down for their naps."

Connor's eyes grew wide. "Naps?"

Laramie and Jack laughed.

"Babies take naps, little dude," Jack said. "Sometimes two or three a day."

"Yuck." Connor craned his neck and pointed behind Jack. "Horse!"

Jack winced. He'd meant to throw a blanket over that thing.

"Did you build that?" Laramie asked.

Jack nodded, feeling the weight of her curious stare as he turned and followed Connor over to the wooden rocking horse. Connor reached out and carefully touched the mane made of floppy strands of gray yarn. Jack shoved his hands in his back pockets and wrestled with the memories that came flooding back. His father and Uncle Kenny had supervised while he cut out the shapes with the saw, then pieced them together, and sanded and stained the wood for hours, until the horse was a beautiful golden brown. Jack's muscles had ached for a few days afterward, but he'd been so proud of the finished toy.

Until Drew had teased him that rocking horses were for babies.

Jack had left the rocking horse in the woodshop instead of entering it in the woodworking contest at the county fair like he'd planned.

"I ride?" Connor's sweet voice interrupted his thoughts.

Jack hesitated. If Connor rode the horse, would he want to keep it? Jack needed to get it out of there, but Gage and Skye might not want something that large in their house. Especially now that their family was growing.

"Pwease?" Connor patted the wooden seat with his little hand then glanced over his shoulder.

"It's a beautiful rocking horse." Laramie shifted Macey to her other hip. "You're very talented."

Her compliment softened the raw places inside. His gaze locked on hers. Questions lingered in those beautiful green pools. A current zinged between them. He longed to lean in and kiss her again.

"Thanks." He forced himself to look away. Connor was hopping in circles around the rocking horse. Jack didn't want to think about what might happen if he didn't keep a close eye on the curious little boy.

Laramie was beautiful, thoughtful and devoted to caring for her family and friends. Knowing she believed in him buoyed his confidence.

But it wasn't enough.

She regretted their kiss. He couldn't stay in Merritt's Crossing, constantly feeling like a disappointment. And he wasn't going to stick around and watch her fall in love with someone else.

Charlotte screeched, reminding them that she was still in the baby swing. Macey was babbling and had grabbed a fistful of Laramie's hair.

"Ride? Pwease?" Connor ran toward Jack, took his hand and tugged him over to the rocking horse.

"I'll put the babies down for their naps," Laramie said, raising her voice above the noise.

"All right, we'll be in soon," Jack called over his shoulder.

While Laramie buckled the girls into the double stroller he'd used to bring them out to the shed earlier, Jack helped Connor onto the rocking horse and showed him how to hold on to the wooden pegs on either side of the horse's head.

Connor laughed as the wooden animal glided back and forth. Jack couldn't help but smile. Although he was glad his nephew was having fun on the rocking horse he'd made, Connor's happiness wasn't enough to make Jack change his mind. He already had a job in a field he enjoyed. The furniture business had its ups and downs, while cybersecurity was very stable. He was weary of wrestling with everyone else's unmet expectations. It was time to start over in a new town with a clean slate.

Chapter Twelve

He was packing.

Laramie couldn't believe it. Jack was really going through with moving. Did he even have a job offer yet? She was afraid to ask. Good thing she'd brought Connor along as a distraction today. Then she didn't have to think about how much it hurt to see the boxes stacking up in the woodshop.

She was supposed to be proud of Jack for finally going into the building. She'd been so excited when Connor discovered the beautiful rocking horse, and she'd hoped the little boy's enthusiasm for something Jack had made might boost his confidence.

But apparently, she was wrong, because he'd looked irritated instead. When she'd complimented him, the doubts lingering in his eyes were impossible to ignore.

"Connor, are you finished eating?" Laramie tapped the edge of his plate with her finger. She'd fixed his favorite—apple slices with peanut butter, cheese cubes and crackers.

"Uh-huh." He shoved his plate away and grabbed his sippy cup.

"Would you like anything else to eat?" Jack stacked his empty plate on top of Connor's, then reached for hers.

"No, thank you." She handed him her plate. "Thanks again for lunch."

"You're welcome." He carried their plates to the sink while Connor noisily gulped down his water.

"I can't believe Macey and Charlotte are still sleeping." She glanced at the time on her phone. It was almost one o'clock. Skye wanted Connor home by two for his quiet time.

"Must be all that fresh air," Jack said.

"Wet's go." Connor slid from his chair and darted past Laramie toward the plastic box of toys Skye had sent with them.

Laramie smiled and followed him to the living room. While she was probably supposed to help him pronounce his letters correctly, she secretly hoped he kept messing up his L's for a little while longer. He was so adorable.

"What's in the box?" She sat in the middle of Jack's carpet. "Any dinosaurs or crocodiles in there?"

"No." Connor laughed and sank to his knees beside her.

"How about a sailboat or a kitten?"

More contagious little-boy laughter bubbled up. Laramie's heart squeezed. Connor had tons of energy and kept his parents on their toes, but he was also so sweet and curious, and she loved seeing the world from his perspective. Kids were the best. Would she ever have any of her own?

Jack came and sat down beside her on the floor. His

knee bumped against hers as he reached in and pulled out Connor's plastic dump truck and cement mixer.

"Connor, what are we building today?"

Oh. She wasn't emotionally prepared for this very domestic setting. "Don't you have to work this afternoon?"

"Are you trying to get rid of me?"

"No, of course not."

Jack leaned back and grabbed a stack of hardcover books from his bookshelf.

Laramie couldn't help but stare as his T-shirt stretched taut across his broad shoulders.

He turned back around, and she pretended to be extremely interested in the rest of Connor's toys.

Connor was busy pressing every button on Macey and Charlotte's baby toy, watching intently as the lights blinked and corresponding musical notes played.

"I have a conference call at two thirty." Jack built a simple ramp for the trucks. "And I'm waiting for an update from one of my project managers."

"I can hang with Connor." Laramie shifted slightly to create space between them. "I'm supposed to take him home for his n-a-p by two o'clock."

"I know." Jack met her gaze. "That's why I'm taking advantage of the opportunity to hang with two of my favorite people."

Her skin flushed and she looked away. "Connor is pretty fun."

"You have your moments, too."

Laramie arranged Connor's matchbox cars in a neat row and ignored Jack's comment. He was flirting again. Wasn't he? They'd been friends for so long, and the time she'd spent with him while caring for his girls had smashed her resolve to avoid falling for a guy who'd behaved so recklessly. If she was one of his favorite people, why was it so easy for him to uproot and leave? And was she willing to hear the answer if she asked?

Before she could formulate the question, someone knocked on Jack's front door.

"Are you expecting a visitor?"

Jack shook his head and stood.

"Who is outside?" Connor followed Jack toward the door. "Can I answer it?"

Jack peeked out the window. "It's Grandma and her…friend."

Connor gasped. "Grandma and Mr. James are *here*?"

Laramie smiled, but she didn't miss the muscle knotting tight in Jack's jaw or the stiffness in his shoulders as he opened the door.

"Hi, Grandma. Hi, Mr. James." Connor bounced up and down in the entryway. "What are you doing here?"

Mrs. Tomlinson's eyes widened. "Well, Connor, hello. This is a fun surprise."

"What's in the box?" Connor stopped bouncing long enough to crane his neck to see what his grandmother held in her hands.

"Hello, Mother. James." Jack's tone was as frigid as a mid-December morning. "Come on in."

"Thank you." Mrs. Tomlinson stepped inside, smiling when she saw Laramie. "Hi, sweetie. James and I thought we'd stop by and bring dinner."

"It's only one thirty." Jack gently closed the door. "We just finished lunch."

Mrs. Tomlinson's smile wobbled. "It's enchilada casserole. You can bake it whenever you're ready. Forty-five minutes at 375 degrees."

"That sounds amazing." Laramie's mouth watered. Mrs. Tomlinson's enchilada casserole was delicious and much more appetizing than the boring salad she'd planned on eating for dinner by herself.

"Here's chips, salsa and your mother's fabulous chocolate chip cookies," James said, gesturing to the brown grocery bag in his arms. "Nice to see you again, Jack. We didn't get to talk much at your birthday party."

Jack quickly shook James's outstretched hand, then crossed his arms over his chest. "Yeah, it was a busy night."

Laramie shot him a meaningful look. *Be nice.* He was clearly irritated and doing a lousy job of hiding it.

"What did you bring me, Grandma?" Connor tugged on her arm.

"Sweetie, I didn't know you were here." Mrs. Tomlinson frowned. "Want to help me take this food into the kitchen?"

"Nope." Connor eyed James. "Did you bring me anything?"

"Connor," Laramie warned. Skye and Gage wouldn't be pleased with his manners right now.

"As a matter of fact, I did." James reached into his grocery bag and pulled out a book with a dump truck, fire engine and police car splashed across the front.

"Wow, look at that." Jack's tone was borderline snarky. "Do you like sticker books, Connor?"

"Yep." Connor clutched the book and examined the cover.

"What do you say?" Laramie prompted.

"Thank you." Connor grinned up at James.

"You're welcome, buddy." James ruffled Connor's hair.

Laramie checked the time on her phone. While she

was tempted to stick around and ease the friction simmering between Jack, his mother and James, she'd promised Skye she'd have Connor home in time for his nap.

"Connor, grab your water cup and let's go show your mom that awesome new book." Laramie quickly packed his toys and shouldered the small backpack he'd brought along.

"Wait. You're leaving?" Jack's brows sailed upward. "The girls are about to wake up and they'll need to eat."

"Your mom and James are here, I'm sure they'd be happy to help with Macey and Charlotte."

"Of course we would." Mrs. Tomlinson stood next to James and slipped her arm around his waist. "Show us what to do."

"But I have a meeting," Jack said.

"And I promised Skye I'd bring Connor home." Laramie slung her purse onto her other shoulder. "He needs his quiet time."

"We understand." Mrs. Tomlinson smiled at Laramie. "Connor, give Grandma a kiss."

He ran into her outstretched arms, still clutching the sticker book.

"See you next time, pal," James called after them as Laramie strode toward the door with Connor at her heels.

"I'll be back soon." She felt the weight of Jack's hard stare as she left. Normally, she'd cave to his not-so-subtle hints to stick around and help. Especially since he got upset when she left to help her grandparents the other day. Not this time, though. Jack's inability to cope with his mother's new boyfriend was not her problem to solve.

* * *

She'd left him. Again.

Jack stared at the door as it closed gently behind Laramie and Connor. He was irritated that she'd left. And angry with himself for being irritated. Laramie didn't owe him a thing. After all, he wouldn't have weathered these first weeks of parenthood without her by his side. Sure, he could've hired a stranger to be a nanny, but it wouldn't have been the same. His feelings for Laramie had morphed from friendship to something much deeper, and he was running out of time to convince her that a relationship with him was not a mistake.

"Jack, how's the internet security business?" James clapped him on the shoulder.

The contact yanked Jack back to reality, and he glanced at James. "Good. Really good. That's why I need to get back to work while the girls are still asleep."

"Not so fast," his mother said. "I hear them waking up."

"No." Jack strode toward the kitchen counter to check the monitor for himself. Macey's and Charlotte's eyes were both open and they were wiggling around in their crib. He should've known their extra-long nap would end as soon as Laramie left. It was almost like they knew he needed them to sleep longer and refused to comply.

"Show me your usual lunch routine and I can help you," his mom said.

Jack pulled the can of formula out of the cabinet along with baby food, spoons and plastic bowls.

James followed them into the kitchen and stood on the opposite side of the counter. "You know, my son is interested in the industry. He's a—"

The spoon slipped from Jack's hand and clattered against the granite countertop. "You have a son?"

James smiled proudly. "I do. A daughter, as well. They both live in Boise, Idaho. Maybe we can all get together soon and introduce you."

Jack's mother smiled at James. "That would be wonderful."

No, it would not, Jack wanted to argue. Instead, he clamped his mouth shut and carefully filled both bottles with warm water. He wasn't naive. If he ever married, his daughters might be part of a blended family. But somehow that seemed different than meeting his mother's boyfriend's adult children now. Jack wasn't prepared for this new season in his mother's life.

"Remember how to make formula?" He popped the lid off the container and fished the scoop out of the powder.

"I think so." Mom lifted her glasses from the top of her head and slid them into place. "You make the first bottle and I'll make the second."

Macey and Charlotte were both crying now. Anxiety hummed in Jack's veins. He really wished Laramie was here. She was so good at multitasking.

"Your mom told me you work for a small firm. Do you prefer that over being self-employed?" James asked.

Jack shook the bottle of formula with a vengeance while Macey's wailing grew louder. He didn't want to be rude. He really didn't. But did this guy not have a clue how hard it was when two hungry babies were both crying?

"You know, I'd love to talk with you and your son about this but—"

"Sweetheart," his mom interrupted. "Would you

mind going and picking up one of those sweet babies? You don't have to change a diaper. Just pick her up and hold her. Either one, it doesn't matter."

His mom couched her instructions with a gentle smile. James's gaze toggled between Jack, Jack's mother, the baby monitor on the counter, then back to Jack's mom.

"No problem," James said. "I'm happy to help."

"Thank you," Mom said sweetly.

"A little-known fact. I'm great at helping crying babies," James called over his shoulder as he strode down the hall toward Charlotte and Macey's room.

Jack's mother shot him a nervous glance. "Are you all right?"

He set the bottle on the counter, then unscrewed the caps on the jars of baby food. "I'm great. Never better."

"He's irritating you, isn't he?"

"No, what gave you that idea?"

"You seem agitated. I mean, you became a father of twins recently, so I understand your anxiety and frustration, but you seem out of sorts. More so than usual."

Jack gripped the edge of the counter with both hands, trying to draw a deep, calming breath.

"You're doing a great job, by the way." His mom's gentle hand on his arm did little to soothe him. "The babies are thriving. This would be hard for anybody and you have handled the transition so well."

"Laramie has handled it really well. I'm a total screwup as usual."

Mom hesitated. "Now, why would you say that? Both girls are healthy and growing. They seem like they've adjusted to all the upheaval. And I know I'm biased because I'm your mother, but you are not a total screwup."

He didn't want to get into this. Not right now. Maybe not ever, but he couldn't keep sidestepping this conversation with his mother, especially since he'd already talked to Drew about it. "Mom, you know Dad and I had a terrible disagreement the day he died. I never wanted to be like him. I said I never wanted any part of the furniture business. Then hours later he was dead."

Mom's eyes widened. "Of a heart attack, honey. Your dad died of a heart attack while he was driving, which caused an accident. Not because of anything you said or did or didn't do."

"I'm a hundred percent certain our argument contributed to his stress."

"And I'm a hundred percent certain that he swindled your uncle out of thousands of dollars. He was on his way to the furniture market to try to sell everything in his truck to pay back loans that he owed creditors. Your disagreement was a terrible situation, and I hate that those were your last words to your father, but you are not responsible."

Jack's breathing grew shallow. He couldn't do this. Not with the babies crying and his mom and James here. "I appreciate you saying that, but I don't think I'll ever be able to forgive myself for what happened."

"Then stop trying to handle it on your own and ask the Lord to help you," she said.

Jack pushed away from the counter and faced her. "What I mean is I think it would be best if the girls and I moved away. If my next interview goes well and I get an offer, I'm taking a job in Utah."

She stared at him in stunned silence. "If that's what you think is best."

He studied her for a long moment, unsure of what to

say. Was it really that easy? She wasn't going to argue with him or try to talk him out of leaving?

"I'd better go help James change those diapers." He brushed past his mom and strode down the hall toward the girls' room. While he felt relieved that he'd shared some of his emotional anguish, his mother's reaction had done nothing to ease his guilt. He'd been a fool to think talking about his feelings might finally set him free. Would he ever be able to escape the grief and regret?

The fragrance of lavender-scented baby shampoo filled the warm bathroom as Laramie finished bathing Charlotte. Across the hall in the girls' bedroom, she heard Macey babbling as Jack—hopefully—was putting her into her pajamas.

"Come on, cutie patootie." Laramie lifted Charlotte from the bath and gently wrapped her in the fuzzy green towel with the frog face on the hood.

"Ba-ba-ba," Charlotte cooed as Laramie placed her on the striped throw rug on the bathroom floor. Water droplets still clung to her eyelashes and she kicked one chubby leg free from the towel while Laramie reached for the bottle of baby lotion. She smiled and Charlotte grinned back, sending a warm rush of affection straight through Laramie's heart.

"You are so adorable." Laramie put on Charlotte's clean diaper, then walked her fingers across her bare tummy and gently tickled her under the chin. Charlotte's blue eyes gleamed and she giggled, an infectious sound that prompted Laramie to repeat the delightful interaction.

She walked her fingers across Charlotte's tummy

again, this time deliberately going slow. The baby's eyes grew wide and she squealed with anticipation. Laramie chuckled, too.

"What's going on in here?" Jack stood in the doorway with Macey in his arms and a smile curving one side of his mouth.

"Check this out." Laramie tickled Charlotte again, provoking more squeals and bubbly laughter. Macey giggled, too, then shoved her finger in her mouth, kicking her leg against Jack's stomach as she watched.

"Thanks for staying longer and helping with their baths." Jack shifted Macey in his arms. "I appreciate the extra set of hands."

"No problem." Laramie slathered lotion on Charlotte's skin. "Especially when I get baby giggles as my reward."

"I'll fix their bottles." Jack's footsteps echoed on the hardwood floor in the hallway as he strode into the kitchen.

Laramie stared after him. He'd been unusually quiet since she came back from taking Connor home. Was he still aggravated about his mother and her boyfriend stopping by unannounced? Had they said something to upset him? She didn't want to pry, but his melancholy mood was evident in the slump of his shoulders and the perma-crease in his brow. She missed his usual good-natured teasing.

"Let's get you dressed, sweet girl." Charlotte resisted, twisting and arching her back while Laramie tried to tuck the squirming baby into the purple-striped pajamas.

"Whew." Laramie zipped up the one-piece, snapped the flap in place so Charlotte couldn't undo her zipper, then picked her up. "Bathing you is a workout, girlfriend."

Charlotte caught her own reflection in the mirror and blew raspberries. Laramie chuckled, hung up the damp towel on the hook behind the door, then carried the baby into the kitchen.

Jack handed her a warm bottle of formula.

Charlotte leaned forward, both arms outstretched, gasping little shallow breaths in anticipation.

"Oh my." Laramie let her hold the bottle. "Let's go sit down."

Jack followed her into the living room and they both sat on the sofa and settled the babies in their laps for the last feeding of the day. Her body was weary from the physical exertion of bathing both girls, and the constant worrying about Jack, his choices and her grandparents' health added another layer of exhaustion. As she sank into the leather cushions and savored the warmth of a sweet-smelling baby nestled in her arms, Laramie let herself relax and her imagination roam.

She imagined this was an ordinary evening—feeding the babies together, then tucking them in. She imagined the handsome guy beside her making her heart do cartwheels with the way he stared lovingly at his daughter wasn't just a friend she was helping for only a few more days. In her wildly creative mind, she imagined she didn't have to leave after the girls were in bed. That this was her home. And they were a family.

"Laramie?" Jack's voice saying her name pulled her back to reality. "Hmm?"

He angled his head toward Charlotte. "She's asleep already."

"Oh." She glanced down at the baby in her arms. The

bottle was barely half-empty, but it had slipped from Charlotte's mouth and her eyes were closed. Laramie stared, certain she'd wake up and cry if she couldn't finish the bottle. Instead, Charlotte drew a deep breath, then released it in one long contented sigh.

"I'll put her in bed," Laramie whispered, her legs brushing against Jack's as she moved past him. Walking slowly down the hallway toward the girls' bedroom, Laramie kept her gaze locked on Charlotte's face. There were plenty of times in recent weeks where she'd tried to tuck her in, and the baby's eyes had popped open as soon as her backside touched the crib mattress. Then they'd start over with the cuddling and the bottle and even gently rocking until Charlotte settled down again. Laramie was not interested in repeating that vicious cycle tonight. All she wanted was a few quiet moments with Jack to talk and make sure he was all right. As a concerned friend. Nothing more.

Jack came into the room behind her and gently eased Macey into the crib beside Charlotte. Then they stood completely still, both listening to the babies. Laramie held her breath. Was this the rare evening where both girls went to sleep at the same time without resistance? Could they be so fortunate?

Jack gave her two thumbs up, then turned and tiptoed out of the room. Laramie followed, pausing to turn on the white noise machine and cast one more glance toward the babies.

When she stepped into the hallway and pulled the door closed, Jack was waiting, his muscular frame blocking her path and those amazing blue eyes locked on hers. He reached up and tucked a loose strand of hair behind her ear.

Her body hummed as his fingertips skimmed her cheek. Oh. She swallowed hard, unable to move.

"Want to stay and watch a movie?"

No. Yes. She should go. But oh, how she wanted to stay. It was impossible to think clearly with Jack standing so close, those smooth, kissable lips only inches away.

"I have a whole carton of chocolate chip ice cream." His eyebrows lifted. "And you can pick the movie."

"Well, you really know how to sweet-talk a girl, don't you?"

His wide smile made her insides dance like wheat swaying in the field. Then his eyes deepened to a shade of indigo like the evening Colorado sky and he angled his head slowly toward hers. Laramie's pulse fluttered in her throat as his gaze slid toward her lips. Instead of taking a step back, her hands found their way to the soft cotton of his gray T-shirt and she rested her palms on his chest. Jack's breath was warm on her skin as his lips parted and she tipped her chin up, no longer able to resist the anticipation of kissing him again.

His lips were soft—softer than she remembered—and she twined her hands at the nape of his neck as he pulled her close and deepened the kiss. The warmth exploding in her chest and Jack's strong hands splayed across the small of her back chased away all her doubts and worries about the future. Just this once, she let herself get lost in the moment.

Jack trailed kisses along Laramie's jaw. A delicious sound slipped from her throat and he relished the sensation of holding her. She was here. In his arms. The girls had stayed asleep. He let his lips linger near her ear, then forced himself to pull away.

"Laramie," he whispered, resting his hands on her waist.

"Hmm?" Her eyelids were heavy and her lower lip full. And tempting. One subtle dip of his chin and he could kiss her again. He managed to hold back, though.

Don't ruin a perfect night by talking about the future.

His thoughts were at war.

If he didn't speak up while he had the courage, he might not get another opportunity before she left for volleyball camp. And after a kiss like that, his heart couldn't handle being in limbo.

"Come with us to Utah."

Her eyes widened and she stepped back. "What?"

Okay, so maybe that was too direct. He'd never been good at greasing the skids before broaching a tough topic. The electricity that arced between them only moments before had been snuffed out.

She wrapped her arms around her torso and rubbed her palms along her upper arms. "I have a job. A team to coach. My family is here. I—I don't want to move."

"That kiss doesn't change your feelings at all?" He hated the irritation that crept into his tone. See? This was what happened when he gave into his emotions. They came crashing into the conversation like an angry bull, stomping out any fragile peace he'd established.

"Our kiss was incredible." Laramie's voice shook. "I'm just being honest."

"You won't be alone in Utah. The girls and I will be there, too."

"But you work, and I'll need a job, too. The girls will be in day care. We wouldn't see each other very often."

He turned away, gritting his teeth against the frustration her words churned up. Why couldn't she understand his perspective? He wanted her to come with him. He wanted her to be a part of his new life with his daughters in Utah. More than anything, he wanted to convince her that tonight was only a glimpse, a small taste, of what was possible between them.

"I respect your parents, and your desire to be close while your grandfather isn't well. On the other hand, don't you think they have the support they need from your brother and the community?"

Even in the late-evening light coming through the kitchen window, he sensed her fierce gaze.

"You know as well as I do that Landon won't help care for my grandfather. Or anybody other than himself."

Her frigid tone should've served as a strong warning. He'd known her long enough to know bringing up Landon was a weak argument. *Don't go there. Just don't.* Yet he couldn't hold back. Wouldn't hold back. There was too much at stake.

Jack faced her again, his heart pounding. "You know, someday you're going to have to choose your own happiness over what's best for other people."

"Like you're doing?" Laramie asked. "Why are you really moving to Utah, Jack? Is living here really that horrible that you just can't stand it?"

Her words knifed at him. "I told you, it's a government job. Great benefits, no more traveling."

"And no family within a day's drive and no friends. Apparently, that's the way you like it."

"Oh, so just because I don't want to stay in the same town where everybody is always gossiping about my family and telling me how I should live my life, that makes me the bad guy?" His voice was rising, and he was fighting for control, but he didn't care. They'd just shared a mind-blowing kiss. And she was too afraid to admit she was scared.

"Why are you doing this?" Her voice broke. "Why?"

"Because I want you in my life, Laramie. Not because we've been friends forever. Not because you're great with my girls. I want *you*." He pushed his tongue in the pocket of his cheek, wrestling against the emotion clogging his throat. "I thought after what happened tonight, you wanted me, too."

"I can't believe you're doing this." She shook her head and brushed past him. A tear glistened on her cheek.

"What? Fighting for you? Trying with everything I have to prove how much you mean to me?"

"You're not fighting for me. You're calling me a coward. Thanks for that." She marched into the living room, grabbed her tote bag and shoved her book, her sunglasses and her water bottle inside. Her keys jangled as she stormed toward the door.

"Wait. Where are you going?"

She paused, her hand on the doorknob, then looked back over her shoulder. Her eyes narrowed into icy emerald pools. "I'm leaving, Jack. Because the only coward in the room right now is you. If you really cared about me and wanted a relationship, then you wouldn't be in such a hurry to drag me away from everything that matters."

Ouch. Didn't he matter? Didn't Macey and Charlotte matter? Jack gritted his teeth to keep any more regrettable words from slipping out.

"Oh, and one more thing." She hovered in the doorway, one foot already out on the porch. "You can find another nanny. I quit."

He winced as the door clicked shut behind her. How had he messed this up so badly?

Chapter Thirteen

Laramie woke up in her childhood bedroom with Bear standing on her stomach and licking her face.

"Ugh, stop." She scrunched her eyes shut against the sunlight glowing behind her striped curtains and gently eased the puppy to the side of the bed. "Puppy kisses are sweet, but not right now."

Trixie raised her head from the end of the bed and blinked slowly, tucking her snout on her paws. She then heaved a sigh and went back to sleep.

If only it were that easy. Laramie yawned and scooped the smaller dog into her arms. "Come here."

Bear whined and twisted against Laramie, squirming to get down. The scent of bacon sizzling in the kitchen teased her senses and made her stomach growl. "That explains why you're trying to get my attention. Thanks for waking me up for bacon."

She lowered him to the floor and eased out from under the covers without disturbing Trixie. As her bare feet touched the shag carpet, Laramie caught a glimpse of her tote bag sagging on the floor by the dresser. Memories from last night came rushing back. The kiss that had made her swoon with happiness, and then the heated words they'd exchanged.

Mortified and shocked that she'd stomped out of Jack's house, Laramie had cried all the way home, then coaxed the dogs into her car and driven to her family's farm. Mom and Dad had welcomed her, offered her hugs, then helped her get settled in her old bedroom.

She rubbed her palm against the hollow ache in her chest. Jack had called her a coward. Why? And she'd hurled ugly words right back. They'd known each other for years and never raised their voices at one another in anger. How had their relationship become so convoluted?

Bear raced out of the room, then turned around and charged at her, tongue lolling. He jumped up and pressed his paws against Laramie's bare knees. When Laramie didn't stand up, Bear yipped impatiently.

"All right, I'm awake. Honest." She stood and rummaged in her closet for her old bathrobe, slipped it on, then followed the puppy downstairs and into the kitchen.

Her mother stood at the stove, humming softly as she turned the bacon in the pan. She was dressed in denim shorts and a flowered blouse, and her pale blond hair was twisted into a neat bun.

Bear leaped off the bottom step, his nails skittering on the linoleum as he raced into the kitchen and pounced on an old stuffed animal lying on the floor.

"Good morning." Mom smiled at Laramie. "Would you like some coffee?"

Laramie nodded and pulled a green mug—a souvenir from a family vacation in Branson, Missouri—from the cabinet above the coffee maker.

"Did you sleep well?"

"Not really."

Mom plated scrambled eggs and added three strips of crisp bacon. "If you're hungry, you may have this."

"Yes, please." Laramie added cream and sugar to her coffee, then padded to the oval table by the window and sat down. Mom set the plate in front of her along with utensils wrapped in a paper napkin.

"Would you like some toast or orange juice?"

"No, thanks." Laramie dug in. "I'm glad Bear woke me up in time to eat. Where's Dad?"

"He and Landon are changing the oil in the tractor." Mom filled her coffee cup and sat opposite Laramie.

Laramie hesitated, a slice of bacon halfway to her mouth. "I didn't realize Landon was still around."

"Sweetie, we hired him to work for us."

No. She finished the bacon and chased it with a sip of coffee, measuring her words carefully. Landon had a lucrative career as a bull rider. Didn't he? Sure, he'd told her he was broke, but she didn't believe him. Hopefully, her parents didn't, either.

"I can see you're not too happy about that news." Mom cradled her coffee in both hands. "What's wrong?"

"I don't understand why a world champion bull rider is back home working on his family's farm. Isn't he supposed to be out on tour or something?"

Mom's features pinched. "We all fall on hard times every now and then. Landon is…regrouping."

Laramie snorted. "Right."

An awkward silence hovered between them. Landon was working an angle. Hatching a plan. He might know how to work on the farm, but she was confident it wouldn't be long before he asked someone in the family for a loan and then disappeared again.

Laramie ate her breakfast while Mom quietly sipped her coffee. Finally, Mom's chair creaked as she sat up straighter, her gaze curious. "Speaking of regrouping, what brings you by?"

Laramie shoveled her fork into the scrambled eggs. Where did she even begin?

"Not that you and your dogs aren't always welcome."

Her heartache brought her here. Where she always wanted to be when life didn't go the way she'd expected. Even though she was a grown woman with a job and a house of her own, when she was hurting, she longed for the comfort of her family and her mother's cooking.

Would that ever change?

"Jack and I kissed," she confessed. "For the second time."

"Oh?" Mom's green eyes widened. "Is that the reason for the tears?"

So she'd heard. Laramie nodded. She'd tried to muffle her crying into her pillow last night. Apparently, it hadn't worked.

"Typically kissing doesn't lead to crying."

"The kiss was great." Laramie's skin heated and she averted her gaze. Her lips still tingled from Jack's touch. The sensation of his warm hands pulling her close wasn't a memory she'd be able to banish anytime soon.

"What else happened that made you upset?"

"He wants to move to Utah and asked me to go, too."

Mom's gasp was audible. "Why don't you go with him?"

Laramie's fork clattered to her plate. "Because I have a job and volleyball season starts soon. Besides, this is my home and I definitely can't move when Grandpa isn't doing well."

"Honey, no one expects you to sacrifice your happiness to take care of the farm or your grandparents."

"You don't?"

"Of course not." Mom rested her hand on Laramie's arm. "Why would you think that?"

"Because I'm always the one who takes care of everyone else."

"That's true." Her mother tilted her head to one side. "And why do you suppose that is?"

Laramie shoved her plate aside and reached for her coffee. "Because you were always too busy with Landon and his bull riding."

Hurt flashed in Mom's eyes. "I was afraid that would happen."

"What do you mean?"

"Your dad and I argued a lot over the years about how much time and attention we devoted to Landon."

Laramie stared into her coffee, surprised by the hot tears pricking her eyelids. "Do you know that Dad never came to even one of my volleyball games?"

"I know," Mom whispered.

"But he never missed a single one of Landon's events."

"It doesn't mean that he doesn't love you."

Laramie couldn't speak around the emotion clogging her throat. She really didn't want to fall apart all over again.

"We can't change the past and I certainly understand why you feel hurt and ignored, but please hear me when I say that you are loved for who you are and not for how you care for others."

"But caring for others is how I show that someone matters to me."

"And you are very loving and attentive," Mom said. "We are grateful for all you do. But we don't expect you to end a relationship with Jack because—"

"We don't have a relationship."

Mom arched an eyebrow.

"We're friends." Laramie sniffed. "We were friends. Now we're not speaking."

"What about the twins?"

"I told him I quit. He'll have to find someone else. I'm leaving for camp the day after tomorrow anyway."

Mom's eyes filled with empathy. "It must've been really hard for you to say goodbye to those sweet babies."

Laramie swiped at her tears with the cuff of her bathrobe sleeve. She'd been so angry with Jack that she hadn't thought about how storming out of his house meant she wouldn't see Macey and Charlotte again for several days. Maybe longer.

"After you and Jack have a couple days to cool off, maybe you can try to work things out."

Laramie sighed. "Doubt it. He called me a coward."

"Oh dear."

"In a totally juvenile move, I called him a coward for wanting to leave town instead of dealing with his guilt over his father's death."

"You were upset. Don't be too hard on yourself."

It wasn't her finest moment.

"I'm sorry to hear Jack still blames himself for his father's death." Mom's brow creased. "Such a tragedy for everyone involved."

"He needs to let it go."

"That's asking a lot, don't you think?"

"Asking me to move to a new place because he can't handle his guilt is unreasonable, too."

Her mother didn't argue, but Laramie sensed by the way she silently sipped her coffee again that she didn't agree.

A wave of uncertainty and regret crashed over her. She'd done the right thing. Hadn't she?

"I'm not moving for a guy unless he proposes, and I'm certain Jack and I aren't ready for marriage."

Mom nodded. "That's a big commitment. Especially since he has two babies. I don't blame you for being cautious."

"I shouldn't have agreed to help him for so long."

"You were generous and kind, taking care of those precious baby girls. There's no reason to regret that."

"Except things ended badly. I'll be fortunate if Jack even lets me see those girls again."

"That's out of your control. Take it to the Lord, sweetie. He knows what you need. Jack and the girls, too."

Laramie heaved a sigh. What she wanted was to snuggle those babies close and savor the warmth of Jack's embrace. But she wasn't moving away again. Not for Jack. Not for anyone.

Man, he wished Laramie was here right now. For a dozen different reasons.

Jack had tried everything. The crying wouldn't stop. He walked through his house with Charlotte pressed against his shoulder. Her cheeks were flushed, and her little blond swirl of hair was plastered to her forehead.

"It's okay, sweet pea." He patted her back with his palm, but she cried and cried, shoving a fist in her mouth. "Are your teeth bugging you?"

He tried to look in her mouth. Charlotte cried harder, arching her back and pushing away from him. What in the world? Panic welled. He had no idea what to do, and Macey wasn't doing much better. She'd started wailing about thirty minutes ago and hadn't stopped. Since he couldn't hold two babies at once, he'd set her in the crib, hoping to be able to help her as soon as he consoled Charlotte.

Except they were both inconsolable.

He strode down the hall to the bathroom and flipped on the light. Maybe there was something in the cabinet that was safe to give babies for teething. Holding Charlotte awkwardly in one arm, he yanked open the top drawer in the vanity cabinet and pawed through the supplies. Tiny nail clippers, toothbrushes, travel-size baby shampoo, but no medicine. He shut the drawer and opened the next one. More shampoo, some lotion and an extra pack of wipes greeted him.

Maybe it was better that there wasn't any medicine. He wasn't sure if they were even old enough to take anything. He closed the drawer, turned off the light and left the bathroom.

There had to be something he could do to get them to stop crying. Sweat dampened his T-shirt and his head throbbed. Then he remembered the teething rings stashed in the refrigerator and strode to the kitchen. Two of the green rings sat on the middle shelf. He took one and offered it to Charlotte. She shook her head and pushed his hand away.

"Come on, sweet girl." He jostled her awkwardly to his other shoulder. She cried louder. If only Laramie was here. She'd know exactly what to do. There was no way he was going to make it through the night with two babies sobbing uncontrollably. It wasn't safe for the girls to cry this much, was it?

He found his phone and called his mother. When she didn't answer, he left a voicemail asking her to call ASAP. Macey and Charlotte kept crying, so he sent his aunt Linda a desperate text as well. A few minutes later, Jack decided he couldn't handle the crying for another second. He sent his mother and his aunt another text, letting them know he was going to the ER, then he tucked the girls in their car seats and drove to the local hospital.

After he parked in the first empty space, he hurried toward the Emergency entrance, struggling to carry both car seats at once. When the automatic doors parted and he stepped inside with two screaming infants, the woman seated at the front desk shot him a wide-eyed stare. Thankfully, she was a high school classmate of Jack's and only a handful of patients sat in the waiting room.

"Come right this way, Jack." She opened the door that led to the exam rooms and motioned him to come through. "If you'll give me your ID and insurance card, I'll send the triage nurse in."

"Thank you." Jack set the car seats down and pulled the cards from his wallet. While he waited for the nurse, he unbuckled the babies and sat on the edge of the exam table, the white paper crackling underneath his weight as he tried to comfort both of his daughters. Their crying had softened some, but that didn't make him feel any better. Something was seriously wrong. He glanced at the clock. There weren't that many people waiting to be seen. Wouldn't the doctor evaluate crying babies first?

"Hello, Mr. Tomlinson." The nurse stepped around

the gray curtain, her rubber clogs squeaking on the speckled gray linoleum floor. "What's going on with these sweet babies?"

"They've been crying for a very long time and I can't figure out why."

"Uh-huh. When was the last time they ate?" The nurse glanced up from the electronic tablet in her hands. With her teal-green scrubs, dark hair in a neat ponytail and calm expression, she looked like a thorough professional who knew how to do her job. But couldn't he share this same information with the doctor, though?

"Mr. Tomlinson?"

"I'm sorry." Dinner felt like weeks ago, instead of just a couple of hours. "I—I tried to feed them their usual food, but they weren't interested. Macey drank some of her bottle. A couple of ounces probably. Charlotte shoved hers away."

"Uh-huh." The nurse tapped at her tablet. "And how many wet diapers have you changed today?"

"Does it really matter?" Jack fought to keep the anger from his voice.

The nurse's eyebrows arched. "We have to take a thorough history, sir."

"They've been crying for hours. That's not normal. And how much longer do they have to cry before you get a doctor in here?"

The nurse set her tablet aside and pulled a stethoscope from the front pocket of her scrubs. "The doctor is seeing another patient right now. She'll be in as soon as she can."

Jack bit back another snide comment and scooted over on the exam table. He kept a hand on Macey while the nurse placed her stethoscope to Macey's bare chest. She screamed louder, her little hands clenched in fists.

This wasn't right. Jack's blood pounded in his head. Charlotte refused to be outdone. Tears slipped from the corners of her eyes as she wailed, her cheeks flushed bright pink. He'd only been taking care of them for a few weeks, but they'd never cried this much.

"Any vomiting or diarrhea?"

"No." Jack raked a hand through his hair. Thankfully.

"And when was the last time you checked their temperature?"

His breath caught. "What?"

"It's possible your daughters both have fevers. You have taken their temperature, haven't you, Mr. Tomlinson?"

Jack squeezed his eyes shut. Their temperature? He didn't even own a thermometer. Did he? And if he admitted that he didn't know how to take a baby's temperature, would the social worker come and take his girls from him?

An icy tingle raced down his spine.

"Mr. Tomlinson?" The nurse stared at him. "Have you taken Macey or Charlotte's temperature today?"

"No." He barely choked out the word.

She sighed. "Well. We'll do that now, then."

"Jack, honey? Are you in here?" His mother peeked around the other side of the curtain in the exam area. Her worried gaze toggled between the nurse, Jack and the twins.

"Mom? What are you doing here?"

"I was driving home from Denver when you called. I'm sorry I didn't answer. When I saw your text, I drove straight here." She frowned and reached for Charlotte. "Come to Grandma, pumpkin."

"Mom—"

"Oh, she is burning up." His mother's eyes widened. "Have you taken her temperature?"

"We were just discussing that." The nurse studied her thermometer. "Macey's temperature is 101 degrees."

"Oh my." Mom patted Charlotte's diapered backside. "How about this one?"

The nurse checked Charlotte next, then glanced at the reading. "This one's 100.2." She updated her tablet, then glared at Jack. "The doctor will be with you shortly."

"Thank you," Mom said, swaying back and forth and pressing her cheek against Charlotte's head.

The curtain rings zinged along the metal bar as the nurse yanked it shut behind her. Jack wanted to throw up. How could he be so clueless?

Aunt Linda appeared on the other side of the curtain.

"Hey," Jack said. "Thank you for coming."

"I'm sorry it took me so long. I was helping Milt mend a fence," she said. "What can I do?"

"Hold her." Mom pointed to Macey. "Jack, why didn't you call the pediatrician? There's always some-one on call."

All he could do was shrug.

His mother frowned and turned away. "We've got to get these babies calmed down. They can have seizures if their fevers get too high."

Seizures? That sounded terrifying. He backed out of the way as his mother and Aunt Linda hovered over the twins.

He was completely useless here. Worse, he'd been so ignorant about taking care of babies that he didn't know he was supposed to check their temperature. Jack swallowed against the sour taste coating his throat.

"I—I—I can't do this." He couldn't breathe. Blood pounded in his head. "I've got to go."

"What?" Mom and Aunt Linda spoke in unison, staring at him wide-eyed. "Go where?"

"Someplace where I can't hurt Macey and Charlotte. Please—" He barely choked out the words. "Take care of them for me, okay? I'll never be enough for them. I'm not meant to be a father."

"Jack, wait." His mother called after him, but Jack turned and fled. Past the triage nurse, past the classmate staring at her computer at the front desk, past the older couple in the waiting room and out into the dark parking lot. Macey and Charlotte never should've been left in his care. He'd messed up and this time his carelessness had endangered his children. He was a horrible father and they were better off with someone who knew how to keep them safe.

Chapter Fourteen

The gym was hot. Stifling hot. Sweat trickled down Laramie's back as she sat on the bleachers and glanced at the clock on the wall. The black hands had only moved two measly minutes since the last time she'd checked.

The air-conditioning had quit working before lunch, and even with the double doors propped open, very little air was circulating. Just two more hours until volleyball camp ended. Then they could load up the vans and drive home.

Except when she envisioned home, all she thought about was sitting in Jack's living room, playing with Macey and Charlotte.

She massaged the ache forming in her head, then took another sip of water from her reusable water bottle as volleyballs flew through the air and bounced across the hardwood floor. The girls were working on their serving and warming up for one more scrimmage. This was usually Laramie's favorite part of camp, but today she just wanted it to be over.

"I'm proud of you." Morgan, her assistant coach,

patted Laramie's arm. "You've been very professional all week."

Laramie offered a weak smile. "Thanks."

She'd tried to be strong. Whenever she thought about Macey, Charlotte and Jack, she'd quickly forced herself to focus on her volleyball team and the purpose of bringing them to camp. They'd worked hard to get to here, with their fundraising and their parents' sacrifices to cover the extra costs. It wasn't fair for her to spend the whole week crabby and distracted over her broken heart. The girls deserved her full attention.

But she couldn't fake her smile all day long. Staying strong every single second exhausted her. When Morgan heard her crying in the room they shared in the university dormitory late at night, Laramie had confessed that she and Jack had had a terrible argument before she left Merritt's Crossing.

What if their rift was beyond repair, and Macey, Charlotte and Jack were out of her life permanently? The realization stung like a volleyball smacking her in the face. And would she ever stop missing Jack and the girls so much?

"Coach?" Hope waved to get Laramie's attention. "Can we practice hitting before the scrimmage starts?"

"Of course." Laramie took one more sip of her water, set her phone on the bleachers, then stood and strode toward the net, determined to be the confident fun-loving coach her girls expected. Morgan brought the cart of volleyballs closer and they both took turns tossing balls into the air while the players formed two lines and ran through the new hitting drill they'd learned this week.

She was only halfway through the drill when her

phone rang. Laramie hesitated. What if it was Jack? Or her mother calling with bad news about her grandfather?

Wait. You're giving the girls your full attention, remember?

"Coach, your phone." Grace gestured toward the bleachers with her thumb. "Want me to get it?"

"Ignore it." Laramie watched as Hope attacked and slammed the ball deep into the court on the other side of the net. "Nicely done, Hope."

Her phone was silent for a few seconds and then started ringing again.

"Coach Chambers?" Grace's features wrinkled with uncertainty. "Are you sure you don't want me to answer that for you?"

"No, thank you." Laramie motioned for the next girl to get ready to hit. "Let's finish this drill and get ready for our scrimmage."

"But what if it's your boyfriend?" Grace teased.

Laughter rippled through the team.

"Very funny." Laramie didn't smile. "I don't have a boyfriend."

Don't let them get to you. She mentally coached herself not to react. Any other time, she didn't mind their good-natured teasing but today doubt shoved its way in. What if Jack or her parents or her grandparents desperately needed her?

You're going to have to choose your own happiness over what's best for other people.

Jack's words echoed in her head. Laramie's breath hitched. She threw the volleyball too close to the net, causing the hitter to rush her approach and spike the ball into the net.

"I'm sorry." Laramie retrieved the ball. "That was my fault. Try again, please."

See, Jack? Look at me, ignoring the phone. How is that for progress?

The girls finished up the drill, retrieved the volleyballs, then circled up with Laramie in front of the bleachers. She gave them quick instructions and encouragement for the scrimmage, then sat down and flipped her phone over without checking the caller ID. While she was proud of herself for trying to stay present in the moment, she couldn't stop the nagging sensation that maybe she should see who called. Morgan was more than capable of coaching while Laramie checked her voice mail.

No.

She'd never tolerate that behavior from Morgan or one of the girls, so it wasn't acceptable for her, either. While her argument with Jack still hurt if she thought about it too much, and she hated that their friendship was probably over, if any good had come from her heartache, she'd learned she wasn't responsible for swooping in and serving everyone else. Especially at the expense of her own needs. She wasn't indispensable. And she didn't have to make herself available all the time for everyone she loved.

Her phone vibrated against her clipboard with a new text message and she was tempted to look. No, she wouldn't. Whatever was happening at home could wait.

The silence was unbearable.

Jack glanced around his extended-stay hotel room, his new home until he found a place of his own, frowning at the sterile brown-and-beige decor. Not a single primary color baby toy in sight. He winced at the memory of Charlotte and Macey's toys scattered across his living room floor, then carefully hung his suit in the hotel room's narrow closet.

Don't think about them. Don't think about home.

In his darkest moments over the last two days, when he'd felt tempted to turn around and drive back home, he'd repeated those same two sentences over and over until the panic subsided.

Or he thought about how helpless and afraid he'd felt in the hospital when the girls had fevers, and that made it easier to convince himself to stay far away from Merritt's Crossing. But in quiet moments like this, a memory would resurface and catch him off guard. While he'd insisted that he wasn't equipped to be a father, there was so much about the twins that he couldn't forget.

Jack pushed the folding door closed and moved on to unpacking the clothes he'd stuffed in his suitcase. The recruiter said the job was his. Tomorrow's final interview was merely a formality. He'd brought his best suit anyway. Part of him couldn't shake the ominous feeling that he'd made a huge mistake, leaving the girls with his mother and fleeing to this new life in Utah.

If a fresh start was the beginning of his life's next chapter, why did he feel so lonely?

Jack crossed the room and stood at the window facing the mountains ringing the city. Wisps of pastel colors painted the evening sky as the sun inched toward setting.

What were Macey and Charlotte doing right now? His throat ached as he imagined his mother putting them to bed. Did Aunt Linda come by and help her? Maybe Laramie had heard what happened and she'd help, too.

"You're an idiot." He pressed his forehead to the glass and stared at the traffic moving through the streets below. Everyone in a hurry to get where they needed to be. People rushing home to have dinner with their families. Tourists on summer vacations with their kids and grandkids.

He missed his daughters so much he could hardly stand it.

Why did he think he'd ever be able to leave them? The constant crying and realization that their high fevers might've led to seizures had wrecked him, but staying in this hotel room and trying to cope with the silence pressing in around him was so much worse.

Jack turned away from the window and sat on the bed. He needed a distraction. Something to occupy his thoughts and keep him from getting back in his truck and driving all night back to Merritt's Crossing. He eyed the remote control but left the television off.

The allure of watching a show uninterrupted didn't offer nearly as much contentment as he'd hoped. It didn't matter if he could watch whatever he wanted when everyone he loved and cared about was a day's drive away. He had the thing he'd longed for—solitude and freedom from judgment. At last, he didn't see the furniture store every day or his dad's friends reminding him of his shortcomings.

But he also didn't see Charlotte's toothy smile or hear Macey's sleepy sigh when he tucked her in at night. And he wouldn't get to spend most days with Laramie anymore. Those incredible green eyes. Her long hair spilling across her shoulders or the curve of her pink lips when she smiled. That contented sound she'd made when he'd kissed her.

Jack pinched the bridge of his nose with his fingertips. Why did he ever think he was better off without her?

Maybe she was better off without *him*.

He stood and found his phone, then scrolled to an app to order takeout for dinner.

All he wanted was to call Laramie and tell her that he'd made a terrible mistake. He was wrong. She was brave and selfless and strong. Her ability to love well was incredible. He was a fool for asking her to move away when living in Merritt's Crossing meant everything to her. She deserved someone who didn't ask her to choose between a relationship and her family. Maybe he was right when he told his mother and his aunt that he'd never be enough. He'd never be enough for Macey and Charlotte. And he'd never be enough for Laramie, either.

"What do you mean he's gone?" Laramie pressed her phone to her ear and let her duffel bag drop to the floor in her entryway. Her heart pounded. Jack *left*?

"He left for Utah while you were at camp," Skye said. "I'm so sorry."

This had to be a misunderstanding. Or a cruel joke. Jack wouldn't leave without saying goodbye. Would he?

"Something terrible must've happened." Hot tears stung Laramie's eyes as Skye's news sank in. Trixie and Bear barked, their claws scratching the glass as they pawed at the back door. The dog sitter she'd hired had left them out in the backyard. Poor things. Laramie strode toward the back door, her legs wobbly like her grandmother's Jell-O salad.

"The girls got sick and Jack couldn't handle it. He took them to the ER because they were both inconsolable. Mom and Aunt Linda went to help him as quickly as they could, and he had a meltdown right there in the hospital," Skye said. "He said he wasn't fit to be a father, that he knew he'd never be enough for Macey and Charlotte."

Oh, Jack.

"Where are the babies?" Laramie whispered.

"They are both with my mother for now."

"But only for a few days, right? Just until he pulls himself together?"

Skye hesitated. "I—I think he wants my mom to be their permanent guardian."

Skye's words wrecked her. Laramie choked back a sob. Those precious babies abandoned all over again. She opened the door and Bear and Trixie barreled inside. Trixie jumped up and pressed her paws against Laramie's waist, tongue lolling as she tried to smother her with kisses. Bear raced toward his bowl and noisily lapped up water.

Laramie sank onto her sofa. "I wish I had answered when he called me."

"This isn't your responsibility," Skye said.

Laramie frowned. "I know, but—"

"You can't rescue him this time."

Laramie's gut clenched. "I'm not going to rescue him."

What did that even mean? Who said anything about rescuing him? She wasn't going to hop back in her car and chase after him like a desperate fool. Spots peppered her vision. She'd just come home from a week at volleyball camp. Jack had dropped his daughters off with his mother and left town. Didn't she have a right to be angry? Or feel the tiniest bit guilty for not answering when he'd called?

Silence filled the air. "I know this is upsetting. We're sad and angry, too. But Jack likes to run from pain. None of us are surprised."

Laramie pulled the phone away from her ear and stared in disbelief. Even though Jack's behavior mirrored his cousin McKenna's when she'd left Connor with Mrs. Tomlinson, Skye's words still cut deep. Maybe Jack's actions didn't surprise his siblings or his mother, but Laramie was completely shocked.

Because she thought she mattered enough for Jack to stay.

Trixie jumped on the sofa and Laramie didn't discourage her. Instead, she sank her fingers into the soft fur on Trixie's head. The dog tipped her snout up and gave Laramie another affectionate lick on the cheek.

"What do you think might happen next?" Laramie asked.

"With the babies? Or with Jack?"

"Both."

"Hopefully, Jack will come home soon. James hasn't proposed yet, but I think he's in love with my mother. And she seems happy with him. His children live in Idaho, so he'll want to travel back and forth. This new season of her life isn't conducive to raising twins."

Laramie squeezed her eyes shut. "The twins need their father. Why can't Jack see that?" There was nothing wrong with being raised by grandparents. Laramie was the person she was today because of her relationship with her grandparents, but Macey and Charlotte would likely struggle with abandonment as they grew up. Having two parents might ease that burden. Laramie longed to help ease that burden. She wanted very much to step in and be that person. The mom they needed.

"My mom is not afraid to ask people to pray. When Jack didn't come back and she had to take the twins home, she started asking everyone she could think of to pray. It seems unlikely, but we are still hoping Jack will change his mind and come home."

"I'm going to pray he comes home, too." Laramie hated to think that their last conversation might've contributed to Jack's decision to leave. She'd spent too much time over the past week mentally rehashing his harsh words. When she was supposed to be working with the girls on their setting technique or refereeing a scrimmage, her thoughts had wandered to Jack's kisses. A hollow ache filled her stomach as she remembered slamming the door behind her. The final punctuation on their heated argument.

"I'll let you know if I hear any updates," Skye said.

"Please. Keep me posted."

"I will."

Laramie ended the call, then pressed her head against Trixie's soft fur. While Jack was an adult and responsible for his own choices, she felt terrible for the things she'd said. And the things she hadn't. She'd been so stubborn and determined to get her way, so convinced Jack's history of making mistakes meant he'd make another one, that she'd been blind to her own flaws.

"Lord, I've been so selfish and prideful. Please forgive me. And if it's not too late, please change Jack's heart. Even if we aren't meant to be, please bring him back to his daughters. They need him desperately."

Chapter Fifteen

Jack's pen hovered over the lease agreement. The one-bedroom apartment he'd found in a new complex was great. Walking distance to his office when the weather was nice. Close to the grocery store and the gym. It was small but offered an incredible view of the mountains.

So why couldn't he sign?

His phone hummed in his pocket and he fished it out. A photo of Macey and Charlotte in their high chairs, smiling with chunks of watermelon in their little fists, filled the screen.

Eating our first watermelon. Wish you were here.

Jack's throat tightened. That photo and eight simple words from his mother propelled him from his chair.

"Is everything okay, sir?" The young woman behind the desk in the apartment's property management office stared at him. "Did you have more questions?"

"No." Jack handed her the pen. "I'm sorry to waste your time, but I've changed my mind."

Her ruby-red lips pursed. "I'm sorry to hear that."

"Again, I apologize." He couldn't stop a smile from spreading across his face. "As it turns out, I'm not meant to be here after all. I need to get back home as soon as possible."

"Thanks for letting me know." She slid the papers toward her. "Safe travels."

"Thank you." Jack strode toward the door and out into the August sunshine. He quickly jabbed at his phone screen and called his mother.

She answered right away. "Jack? Is that you?"

"Hey, Mom." He swallowed hard against the ache in his throat. "I—I messed up. Moving away was a huge mistake. I'm coming home tonight."

Silence filled the line, then he heard her sniffling.

"That's wonderful news, sweetie. I'm so glad." She drew a wobbly breath. "Macey and Charlotte will be so happy to see you."

He squeezed his eyes shut, then cleared his throat. "I can't wait to see all of you."

"Are you leaving now?"

"As soon as I grab my stuff from the hotel." He jogged toward his truck and got in. "Don't tell Laramie, okay? I want to surprise her."

"Of course you do," Mom said. "Your secret is safe with me."

"I'll see you in about nine hours." Jack ended the call, then drove away from the apartment complex. He couldn't wait to get home and kiss his sweet babies. He'd missed them more and more with each passing day. Then he'd find Laramie and tell her he couldn't live another second without her in his life.

He'd finally come to the end of himself. It was time to admit to his family and to Laramie that he had gotten this all wrong. Jack gripped the steering wheel tighter as he merged onto the interstate. Why had he been so stubborn? Worse, he'd let his own hurt blind him to the blessings that were right in front of him the whole time. His stomach twisted as he thought about what his leaving might've done to Macey and Charlotte. Sure, kids were resilient. Connor was proof that a permanent home and a loving family offset early childhood trauma. He still felt horrible for leaving his children.

Thankfully, he'd lasted less than two weeks in Utah, and his mother had patiently waited for him to come to his senses. She was such a selfless person. He had a lot to learn from her.

As the miles stretched before him, Jack shifted in his seat, suddenly compelled to pray. He knew he needed to reconnect with the Lord before he got home and reconnected with his family.

But where to start? Jack palmed the back of his neck, then reached for the knob on the radio to turn up the volume. He'd never been very good at this talking-to-God stuff. And his parents, aunts and uncles—they always made it look so easy. When his grandparents were alive, they'd incorporated their faith into their lives so naturally. Jack wanted that, too.

He turned off the radio, then heaved a sigh in the overwhelming silence of the truck's cab. He felt so awkward and maybe a little bit foolish, but at least he was alone while he tried to reach out to God. Somehow, deep in his heart, he knew that even though he'd messed up all of the relationships with the people in his life that mattered most, his family and the foundation they established for him in church as a little boy had taught him he was never too far gone. He could always run back to the Lord. It was too late to restore his relationship with his earthly father, but if he made things right with his heavenly Father, he knew he'd find peace at last.

Laramie sat down on the sofa with a giant bowl of popcorn for one and a diet soda. She'd normally savor a quiet evening without any commitments before the hectic pace of volleyball season and a new school year kicked in. Tonight she couldn't shake the loneliness blanketing her like an ominous storm cloud.

This was the saddest Friday night of her entire summer. Trixie heaved a sigh and lowered her snout to her paws, her chocolate eyes filled with empathy.

"I know, right?" Laramie grabbed her remote. "This is pathetic."

Bear was sprawled halfway on and halfway off his bed. He barked softly and his tail thumped against the hardwood while he slept.

Laramie scrolled through the channels in search of a movie to chase away her gloomy mood. Maybe she needed an action-packed adventure instead of her usual heartwarming romantic flick.

Before she could choose, her phone rang. Laramie ignored it. She'd given up on Jack calling her, and she didn't want to talk to anyone else. What was he doing tonight? Working late from some trendy new loft apartment with a breathtaking view of downtown Salt Lake City? Or hanging out with his new coworkers?

Did he think of her or his girls at all?

And why did it even matter? He was gone and she hadn't heard from him. That was all she needed to know. She certainly wasn't going to spend another night crying over Jack.

Her phone chimed again, indicating a new voice mail. She craned her neck to see the screen, which was just out of reach on the coffee table. What if Jack was calling?

No. She wasn't going to look. Even if he was calling, she had to be strong and not answer. He had to understand he couldn't toy with her heart like that. She pointed the remote toward the television when her phone rang again.

Guilt swept in. Maybe she should see if the call was important. It might be her mother or a volleyball player or a parent. Laramie grabbed her phone from the coffee table, noted her mother's number on the screen and swiped to answer.

"Hello?"

"Oh, finally. You answered." Mom's voice was breathless. "Laramie, we need your help."

"Mom? What's going on?" Laramie set her bowl aside and pushed to her feet.

"It's your grandfather." Mom's voice broke. "Honey, he's missing."

Laramie gasped. "What? How?"

"We're not sure. Your grandmother thought he'd fallen asleep watching the news, and she went to put some clean clothes away. Then she noticed he wasn't in the living room or anywhere else in the house."

Laramie's heart thudded. "He's wandering around the farm alone?"

Her mother's silence confirmed her worst fear. "Mom, how long has he been missing?"

"We don't know where he is or when he left. That's why I'm calling. There's a Silver Alert issued that will be broadcast on the emergency services network and on the interstate digital signs. That will alert travelers to be on the lookout."

Laramie cupped her hand to her mouth to hold back a sob.

"Your brother and Drew Tomlinson are getting a team together and they'll start searching until we can find him."

She jumped to her feet and motioned for the dogs to get in their crates, grabbed treats from the box and dropped them in with Trixie and Bear, then latched the doors. "Where should I start?"

"There's a team gathering at the farmhouse now," Mom said.

"I'll be there in a few minutes."

"Wear good shoes and bring a flashlight."

"Got it." Laramie ended the call. Her worst fears had become a reality. Her beloved grandpa was missing. She shoved the flashlight, extra batteries and a bottle of water in a canvas tote. Then she tucked her pony-tail in a baseball cap, laced up her tennis shoes and ran out the door.

"Please, please let Grandpa be okay," she prayed as she drove to the farm. It would be dark in a few minutes. Even though it was still warm for a little while after the sun went down, the forecast said temperatures would drop significantly overnight. What if they didn't find him? What if he got cold or thirsty? He was already disoriented or else he wouldn't be missing. She stopped herself from thinking about the unimaginable. They'd find him. They had to.

By the time Laramie pulled up in front of the farm-house, six vehicles were already in the long driveway, including Drew Tomlinson's sheriff's deputy vehicle.

She parked her car beside her brother's truck, grabbed her flashlight and jumped out. The sky had turned a rich indigo blue since the sun had dipped below the horizon. She shivered a little, wishing she'd remembered to grab a jacket.

"Hey, Laramie," Landon greeted her as she joined the circle of men and women forming in front of her grandparents' house. She paused, realizing that she'd never bothered to ask what had brought him back home. The hurt in his eyes and the defeated slump of his shoulders hinted at the heavy burden he carried.

She tucked her arm in the crook of his elbow and squeezed his bicep. "We got this," she said, bumping her hip against his.

Landon swallowed hard, then nodded.

From the lights between the house and the garage, she caught a glimpse of the moisture gathering in his eyes, and she had to look away to keep from bursting into tears. For all her frustration directed at her brother lately, they were united in their cause now. Their shared love for their grandfather and their longing to have him home where he was safe and cared for helped her set their differences aside.

"Let's break up into pairs or groups of three if there's an odd number." Drew handed them all a piece of paper. "Here are some maps of the farm and the adjoining farms on all sides. It's my recommendation that you stay on this side of the highway. The sheriff and another deputy are searching from the other side of the highway out to the interstate. We have a Silver Alert issued along I-70, so work in a grid pattern little by little. You can call his name, but there's no guarantee that he'll respond verbally."

What if the volunteers walked right by Grandpa but he wasn't capable of responding? The horrible thought made Laramie's stomach sink.

"Remember not to panic and frighten him when you find him. Keep your cell phone and your flashlight and a bottle of water on hand. He'll most definitely need to be rehydrated. As soon as he's located, call me immediately. If you don't have my number in your contacts, make sure you all do before you start searching. Any questions?"

The volunteers studied their maps as they paired off. The low hum of conversation filled the air. Laramie glanced at the map Drew had given, even though she and Landon knew this land like the backs of their hands. They'd grown up traipsing through these fields, harvesting wheat and soybeans and corn. The same land their grandfather had grown up on, too.

How could he possibly be lost?

She stared off at the horizon and the red lights on the wind turbines blinking out a steady cadence. "Please come home, Grandpa," she whispered. "We love you."

"Let's go, sis." Landon cleared his throat. "We're going to find Grandpa and bring him home."

The rumble of an engine moving toward them caught their attention. Laramie turned and glanced over her shoulder. Bright headlights illuminated the yard and she squinted to shield her eyes. A familiar truck joined the others in front of her grandparents' house. Her heart pounded.

It couldn't be.

"Is that Jack?" Landon asked.

"I—I think so."

The truck door opened and Jack exited, his profile

silhouetted by the light inside the truck's interior. "Wait. I want to help."

Laramie pressed her fingertips to her mouth as he clicked on his flashlight and quickly scanned the group.

"You can come with us." Landon waved his own flashlight to get Jack's attention.

Laramie didn't know whether to hug her brother or smack him.

Jack strode toward them and stopped a few inches away. In the semidarkness and silvery white light of their flashlights, it was hard to read his expression.

"You're here," she whispered.

"I saw the Silver Alert on the signs on the interstate, then my mom called me when I was driving through Denver. I know we have a lot to talk about, but I'd like to help with the search first."

"What about your girls?"

"Don't worry." Jack's tender smile made her heart expand. "They're in good hands. C'mon, let's go find your grandfather."

She nodded, then turned and followed Landon into the dark fields flanking their farm. This was terrifying, but she didn't have to face the uncertainty alone. And she was overcome with gratitude that Jack had come home to help her and her family.

Laramie stifled a yawn behind her clipboard, then leaned forward on the edge of her metal folding chair on the sideline of the volleyball court. They'd found her grandfather around one thirty this morning, asleep in the cab of a piece of farm equipment out in the shed. She'd been relieved and exhausted, yet she'd still tossed and turned for several hours thinking about what Jack's reappearance meant. They'd gone home without speaking and she'd worked today, still wrestling with so many unanswered questions.

The referee's whistle bleated and signaled for Hope to serve the volleyball. This was a scrimmage, a friendly match before the season officially started. Laramie was still keeping score though, and Merritt's Crossing was up by two points. If they scored, the match would be over.

C'mon, Hope. They'd lost to this team at the end of last season in a heartbreaking match. Although her girls still had a lot of room to improve, she also saw tremendous potential. Winning this scrimmage would boost their confidence.

Three quick bounces on the gym floor, then a toss in the air, and Hope sent the volleyball sailing over the net and deep into the opponent's court. They had their best middle hitter poised for an attack.

Laramie leaned forward and called out instructions. "Defense, ladies." She motioned with her free hand for the defensive specialist to play her position. "We need a big middle block."

Thankfully, the other team struggled to pass the ball to the setter. Their player was caught off guard and had to abandon her plan and set up her weaker outside hitter. The girl's timing was off on her approach and she sent the ball careening out of bounds.

"Yes!" Laramie whooped, jumping to her feet and thrusting both hands in the air, nearly hitting Morgan in the head with her clipboard. Merritt's Crossing had won! While the girls huddled in the middle of the court, Laramie crossed to the other bench and shook hands with the coach.

"Good game."

"You, too," the woman said. "We look forward to a rematch on our court next month."

Laramie offered a polite smile. "Absolutely."

After the players lined up at the net and shook hands, Laramie gathered them in a circle. "Great job, ladies. I'm proud of you. That's the way I want you to play every match. Confident and working together as a team. Hands in and teamwork on three. One-two-three."

"Teamwork." The girls cheered and flung their hands in the air.

"Eat a healthy dinner, get some rest and we'll see you at practice on Monday. Remember we'll start at three thirty."

The girls collected their water bottles and warm-ups, then dispersed into the bleachers to speak with their friends and families. Laramie waved to a handful of teachers who'd come to watch the scrimmage. Just like when she was in high school, she let her gaze scan the bleachers for her parents and Landon. They were all lined up in the second row. She smiled and waved, fighting back unexpected tears.

Finally. They'd come to a game.

Her stomach growled, reminding her that she'd been too nervous about the scrimmage to eat much. She craved a celebratory order of nachos from Pizza, Etc., a post-match tradition that had started years ago. But she wasn't in high school anymore and she hadn't finished getting her classroom ready for the beginning of school yet, so she'd have to settle for a salad at home. Besides, she hated the idea of eating alone.

Laramie pushed the cart of volleyballs into the storage closet, then locked the door and slung her bag over her shoulder. As she strode toward the gym's exit, her steps faltered when she saw Jack leaning against the wall.

A slow smile lifted one side of his mouth. "Great match. Congrats on the win."

"Thank you." She searched his face. "What are you doing here?"

"I heard there was a highly anticipated match featuring an intense rivalry." His eyes gleamed as he pushed off the wall and closed the distance between them. "I couldn't miss it."

And she couldn't think straight with those eyes the color of a mountain lake locked on hers. Her fingers itched to run her hand along the golden stubble clinging to his jaw. Instead, she clenched the canvas strap of her bag. He'd left without saying goodbye. Chosen Utah alone rather than building a life here with her. Even though he'd helped find her grandfather, she wasn't about to fling herself into his arms now.

"Why are you really here, Jack?"

"I'm here for you." His expression grew serious. "I missed you. I missed us. I've had a lot of time to think and I realized I made a mistake, leaving you. Leaving my girls. I'm so sorry. I need you, Laramie. And I want you. Not because I need a nanny or a personal assistant, but because I love you."

Laramie pressed her fingers to her lips as tears blurred her vision.

"Say something." Uncertainty flickered in his eyes. "Don't leave me hanging here."

She reached for his hand. "I love you, too."

The parents and remaining players faded into the

background. Jack's eyes smoldered as he angled his head. "May I kiss you?"

Laramie nodded and closed her eyes, pressing up on tiptoes to meet Jack's lips with her own. She savored the warmth of his mouth moving against hers. When she clutched a fistful of his T-shirt and he deepened the kiss, a whoop of approval echoed around them. She smiled, breaking the kiss, and Jack cupped her face in his and leaned back.

"We'd better settle down," he said. "Forgot there was an audience."

"I didn't," she whispered. "Who cares if they see me kissing the man I love."

In true Merritt's Crossing fashion, the whole town would know in a few minutes anyway.

"And what if they see me ask you a very important question?"

Her breath hitched. Before she could answer, Jack was down on one knee with a velvet box in his outstretched hand.

"Laramie Elizabeth Chambers, you are a gift. The best person I know. I've made a lot of mistakes in my life and I hope you can give me a second chance. I'm kind of a package deal, but my daughters are pretty adorable, so there's that."

Moisture glistened in his eyes and his smile wobbled as he fought for control of his emotions. Laramie's heart pounded like a freight train rolling across the prairie. A hush had fallen over the small crowd huddled in a semicircle around them.

"Will you make me the happiest man in the world and marry me?"

"Yes!" She didn't have to hesitate or overthink or

second-guess her response. Jack slipped the ring on her finger, then pulled her into his arms and twirled her around. The gym erupted in whistles and cheers.

"I can't wait to make you mine," he murmured as he lowered her feet to the ground and his lips hovered mere inches from hers.

Then he kissed her again. She was going to be Jack's wife. Macey and Charlotte's mother. Maybe they'd have a whole houseful of kids. No need to race ahead, though. For now, she let herself get lost in the moment, kissing her future husband senseless.

we watching her leave, and she kept moving on

Epilogue

The doors at the back of Merritt's Crossing Community Church were still closed. A gorgeous Christmas tree filled the opposite corner, glistening with white lights and silver-and-gold ornaments. Inside, the guests had claimed their seats in the sanctuary. The muffled sound of the pianist playing Beethoven's "Moonlight Sonata" made her body hum with anticipation.

Today she was marrying Jack. In a few minutes, she'd be his wife. This was finally happening. Laramie stood in the narthex while Skye made last-minute adjustments to the train of Laramie's wedding gown. She drew a deep breath and smoothed her hand across the beaded bodice. With the short, fitted sleeves and sweetheart neckline, the gown was everything she'd dreamed of. A December wedding was challenging to plan in less than six months. She'd spent many late nights at her parents' house, poring over the details. But she and Jack didn't want to wait any longer. The girls needed a mother and father together in one house. And she couldn't stand to live apart from them for another second.

Laramie's father stood next to her in his black tuxedo. She stole a quick glance. He fought for a smile, but she saw the unshed tears brimming in his green eyes.

"Dad, please don't cry yet," Laramie said. "If you start crying, then I'll start crying—"

"And then we'll all be crying our way down the aisle," Skye said.

Nervous laughter rippled through the bridal party.

Dad cleared his throat. "Give me a minute and I'll pull myself together."

Landon was escorting her mother down the aisle to her seat. Laramie's friend Bethany had come back from Arizona and her cousin Whitney had driven in from Nebraska to be Laramie's bridesmaids. All the people she loved and cared about most in the world were here to celebrate.

The flower girls were adorable in their toddler-sized white dresses with maroon ribbon sashes tied in over-size bows at their waist. Even though Skye was in the last trimester of her pregnancy, she'd been a thoughtful and attentive maid of honor. And she looked radiant in her cranberry-red bridesmaid's dress. Laramie wasn't confident Macey and Charlotte could make it all the way down the aisle to stand up front with them, but she couldn't not include them in the wedding party. If it weren't for the twins, she and Jack might not have fallen in love.

Hope had agreed to corral them and try to coax them down the aisle in the center of the sanctuary. Hope's mom, who was the unofficial wedding coordinator, had Jack's friends in their tuxedos, lined up and ready to go. Except for Jack and Drew, who were already waiting at the altar.

Despite her comment to her father that he couldn't cry, she felt a lump clogging her own throat. Skye fidgeted with Laramie's bouquet while the photographer orbited around, her camera poised in front of her face as she snapped pictures. Laramie had waited so long for this day. She'd never thought she would be a bride. Every year that passed as she moved through her thirties, she was convinced she'd be single forever. While she and Jack had taken the long way around to their happily-ever-after, she wouldn't trade any of it.

Today she would become not only Jack's wife, but Macey and Charlotte's mother, too. While they called her mama and she'd stepped into the role the day they came to live with Jack last spring, it about killed her to go home at night to her own place. Even though she saw them every day, she couldn't wait until they were officially a family of four. No more lingering goodbyes on Jack's porch or driving home at midnight, counting the days until they were husband and wife.

Hope's mom gave them her final instructions, then the back doors of the sanctuary opened. Macey and Charlotte went first, with Connor serving as a dapper ring bearer. He was giving orders to the twins in a loud voice, which sent a ripple of laughter through the guests seated in the back rows. Macey and Charlotte wanted nothing to do with their baskets of flower petals. Hope and her mother offered Laramie an apologetic look, along with helpless shrugs.

Laramie laughed and gave them a dismissive wave. They might be one-year-olds but already they made their preferences clear. Of all the details she'd stressed about and overanalyzed, Charlotte and Macey refusing to throw petals down the center aisle would not faze her. The twins were precious, and she was so grateful to have them in her life.

After Skye started walking, Laramie and her dad stepped into position in the archway. The opening chords of "Here Comes the Bride" began to play and Laramie had to blink back tears. As the rustle of the guests standing to their feet and turning to face her filled the air, her heart soared. She had told herself she wasn't going to look at Jack. Not yet.

That lasted all of two seconds. Unable to resist a glance toward the altar, she saw him waiting for her with his hands folded behind his back, looking incredibly handsome in his tuxedo. She could tell by his expression and the sheen of moisture in his eyes that he was fighting back tears, too.

Golden winter sunlight streamed through the stained glass windows of the church, and while she and her father had agreed they'd walk at a steady pace down that aisle, her legs itched to break into a run. She couldn't wait to start her life with Jack.

She had her hand tucked in the crook of her father's elbow and he reached over with his free hand and gave her fingers a gentle pat.

"Slow down, sweet girl, you're only going to make this walk once," he said.

Laramie felt her grin stretch wide and she forced herself to slow her steps. He was right. She was only going to take this walk once and she wanted to savor every second.

At the front of the sanctuary, her gaze locked with her grandmother's. Laramie could weep with joy at the sight of her grandparents sitting in the second row behind her mother. She didn't know if Grandpa knew where he was or if he was even aware of the significance of this day, but it didn't matter to her. He was there to see her marry Jack and that was enough. Although it wasn't planned, Laramie paused, leaned down and kissed her grandma on her cheek, then reached over and squeezed her grandfather's arm.

"I love you both so much," she whispered. "I'm so glad you're here."

A few moments later, her father lifted her veil, kissed her cheek and joined her hands with Jack's.

"I love you," Jack whispered as they faced the minister, their hands intertwined.

"I love you, too." She smiled and squeezed his hands as they stepped forward into forever and embraced their happily-ever-after.

* * * * *

If you enjoyed this book by Heidi McCahan, pick up
Skye and Gage's story, Their Baby Blessing,
available now from Love Inspired.

Dear Reader,

Often when I'm writing a book, a secondary character shows up in my imagination and quickly becomes an important part of the story. These characters play valuable roles because they help the hero and heroine get where they need to go. Their actions and dialogue are essential for moving the story forward. I can't explain how or why I decide if a secondary character gets the opportunity to become the hero or heroine of a future novel. In Jack and Laramie's case, they showed up in *Their Baby Blessing* and I was glad to make them the hero and heroine of this novel. But I needed help.

Just like characters thrive in their fictional close-knit communities, I needed "my people" more than ever to complete this book. Thank you to my friends and family for cheering me on. Thank you to my fellow Love Inspired authors who encouraged, listened and helped me brainstorm key plot points. A special thanks to Shana Asaro, my editor, for patiently coaching me through the process of shaping Jack and Laramie's story into something worth reading. I'm thrilled that you've helped me send another book into the world.

Thank you, readers, for supporting Christian fiction and telling your friends how much you enjoy our books. I'd love to connect with you.

You can find me online at https://www.Facebook.com/heidimccahan/, http://heidimccahan.com/ or https://www.Instagram.com/heidimccahan.author.

For news about book releases and sales, sign up for my author newsletter at http://www.subscribepage.com/heidimccahan-newoptin.

Heidi